Crime in the Kennel

Frank peered into the darkness.

A compactly built, muscular dog trotted out of the shadows. Frank stopped. He stared transfixed at the dog's electric yellow eyes. It growled menacingly. In the dim light from the open office door, Frank recognized the dog's breed and knew it wasn't Spike.

It was a pit bull.

Suddenly the dog lunged. Frank tried to back out of the way, but he bumped into a broken office chair. He raised his arm too late to fend off the dog's glistening fangs.

In an instant Frank calculated the dog's target. It was going straight for his throat.

The Hardy Boys Mystery Stories

#59 Night of the Werewolf
#60 Mystery of the Samurai Sword
#61 The Pentagon Spy
#62 The Apeman's Secret
#63 The Mummy Case
#64 Mystery of Smugglers Cove
#65 The Stone Idol
#66 The Vanishing Thieves
#67 The Outlaw's Silver
#68 Deadly Chase
#69 The Four-headed Dragon
#70 The Infinity Clue
#71 Track of the Zombie
#72 The Voodoo Plot
#73 The Billion Dollar Ransom
#74 Tic-Tac-Terror
#75 Trapped at Sea
#76 Game Plan for Disaster
#77 The Crimson Flame
#78 Cave-in!
#79 Sky Sabotage
#80 The Roaring River Mystery
#81 The Demon's Den
#82 The Blackwing Puzzle
#83 The Swamp Monster
#84 Revenge of the Desert Phantom
#85 The Skyfire Puzzle
#86 The Mystery of the Silver Star
#87 Program for Destruction
#88 Tricky Business
#89 The Sky Blue Frame
#90 Danger on the Diamond
#91 Shield of Fear
#92 The Shadow Killers
#93 The Serpent's Tooth Mystery
#94 Breakdown in Axeblade
#95 Danger on the Air
#96 Wipeout
#97 Cast of Criminals
#98 Spark of Suspicion

99 Dungeon of Doom
#100 The Secret of the Island Treasure
#101 The Money Hunt
#102 Terminal Shock
#103 The Million-Dollar Nightmare
#104 Tricks of the Trade
#105 The Smoke Screen Mystery
#106 Attack of the Video Villains
#107 Panic on Gull Island
#108 Fear on Wheels
#109 The Prime-Time Crime
#110 The Secret of Sigma Seven
#111 Three-Ring Terror
#112 The Demolition Mission
#113 Radical Moves
#114 The Case of the Counterfeit Criminals
#115 Sabotage at Sports City
#116 Rock 'n' Roll Renegades
#117 The Baseball Card Conspiracy
#118 Danger in the Fourth Dimension
#119 Trouble at Coyote Canyon
#120 The Case of the Cosmic Kidnapping
#121 The Mystery in the Old Mine
#122 Carnival of Crime
#123 The Robot's Revenge
#124 Mystery with a Dangerous Beat
#125 Mystery on Makatunk Island
#126 Racing to Disaster
#127 Reel Thrills
#128 Day of the Dinosaur
#129 The Treasure of Dolphin Bay
#130 Sidetracked to Danger
#131 Crusade of the Flaming Sword
#132 Maximum Challenge
#133 Crime in the Kennel

Available from MINSTREL Books

133

The HARDY BOYS®

CRIME IN THE KENNEL

FRANKLIN W. DIXON

A MINSTREL® BOOK

PUBLISHED BY POCKET BOOKS

New York   London   Toronto   Sydney   Tokyo   Singapore

This book is a work of fiction. Names, characters, places and incidents are products of the author's imagination or are used fictitiously. Any resemblance to actual events or locales or persons, living or dead, is entirely coincidental.

A MINSTREL PAPERBACK *Original*

A Minstrel Book published by
POCKET BOOKS, a division of Simon & Schuster Inc.
1230 Avenue of the Americas, New York, NY 10020

Copyright © 1995 by Simon & Schuster Inc.

Front cover illustration by Vince Natale

Produced by Mega-Books, Inc.

ISBN: 0-671-87217-6

First Minstrel Books printing August 1995

10 9 8 7 6 5 4 3 2 1

THE HARDY BOYS MYSTERY STORIES is a trademark of Simon & Schuster Inc.

THE HARDY BOYS, A MINSTREL BOOK and colophon are registered trademarks of Simon & Schuster Inc.

Printed in the U.S.A.

Contents

1. The Dog-Sitters   1
2. Off Ramp to Danger   13
3. The Cats versus the Dogs   20
4. Who Was That Masked Man?   30
5. Hit-and-Run   40
6. Kibbled to Bits   50
7. 4B or Not 4B?   59
8. A New Paint Job   67
9. Lowering the Boom   77
10. Death Threat   85
11. Roll Over and Play Dead   93
12. Every Dog Has Its Night   100
13. Noises in the Dark   110
14. Out of Her Misery   118
15. Put to Sleep   126
16. Here a Dog, There a Dog   134

CRIME IN
THE KENNEL

1 The Dog-Sitters

"Iola's on the phone," eighteen-year-old Frank Hardy called, lowering the receiver from his ear. "She was just fired from her job at the kennel," he added, disbelief in his voice. Frank held the phone out as his brother approached.

Joe Hardy, a year younger than Frank, ran his hand through his blond hair. Iola Morton was Joe's girlfriend. If Iola was in trouble, he had to help her.

Joe took the phone. "What's going on?" he asked Iola.

"I'm at work," she said, her voice trembling, "at the pet motel. Somebody stole a champion collie from the kennel, and the police are asking me a lot of questions. My boss is really upset. He keeps

1

implying that I might have had something to do with it. You've got to come help clear this up. Officer Riley is here. I'm sure he'll believe you."

Con Riley, of the Bayport Police Department, knew the Hardys well. Joe and Frank were responsible for solving a number of mysteries that had baffled the police.

"Don't worry, Iola," Joe said. "We'll find the real thief."

Frank hadn't heard what Iola said, but the look in his brother's blue eyes meant that Joe was concerned. "You can tell me what this is all about on the way," Frank said after Joe hung up.

Frank took a moment to leave a note for their aunt Gertrude, letting her know where they'd be. Fenton and Laura Hardy, the boys' parents, were away at a conference, and Gertrude Hardy was keeping an eye on things.

The Hardys trotted outside to their van, which was parked in the driveway. "Iola took that job as day manager this summer because she thought working with animals would be fun," Joe said as Frank slid behind the wheel. "But being called a thief sure can take the fun out of it." While Frank headed up High Street, Joe filled him in on Iola's situation.

The Doghouse Pet Motel was on the north edge of town. Frank chuckled when he saw the building: it looked like a real motel. There was even a neon sign reading Vacancy.

2

The driveway circled under a large portico. Frank pulled in, then stopped across from the main office. He could see Iola, Con Riley, and some other people through the front windows.

Joe was out of the van before Frank had shifted into Park. He pushed open the glass door and hurried behind the registration counter, where Iola stood. Frank nodded a greeting to Officer Riley and stood at the entrance.

"Now, who's this?" a tall man with salt-and-pepper hair demanded. He slapped a hand on the registration counter.

"I'm Joe Hardy," Joe said in a businesslike tone, "and this is my brother, Frank." Their names obviously meant nothing to the man. He just glared at the two detectives.

"You two are really the Hardys?" an excited voice asked. Joe looked past the angry man to a young woman about his own age who had entered the reception area from the back. He couldn't help noticing that her long brown hair needed brushing and her clothes were wrinkled.

"Wow," she said. "I read about you guys in the *Banner*. The way you busted those thieves at the carnival was pretty cool."

"This is Dana Bailey," Iola told Joe. "Dana's the night manager."

Dana squeezed past the tall man and shook hands, first with Joe and then Frank. "You'll have to excuse my appearance," she said apologetically.

She tugged at her wrinkled blouse. "I was sound asleep when Mr. Price called."

"Someone has to fill in," the tall man said, "since Iola won't be working here any longer."

"That's not fair!" Iola told him. "I had nothing to do with the theft."

"Maybe not, but my wife and I own the Doghouse," he said, crossing his arms. "I can hire and fire anyone I want." Then, looking at Frank and Joe, he added, "I'm George Price."

Con Riley stepped forward. "My initial investigation," he told the group, "leads me to believe the thief came in through a door in the kennel. I found marks indicating the lock had been jimmied."

Joe asked if he and Frank could look around.

"If anyone can find out what happened to the collie," Dana Bailey spoke up, awe in her voice, "they can. They're actually famous!"

Joe smiled at Dana's compliment and then followed Officer Riley through the door into the kennel. The rest of the party trooped along behind them.

Joe could see that the cages along both walls were for larger dogs. Smaller cages, lined up on shelves above, were perfect for Pekingese, Shih Tzu, and other small breeds. The dogs began to bark as the group approached. Dana spoke soothingly to the animals, handing treats through the bars. Joe noticed that many of the cages were empty.

Joe followed Riley down the narrow aisle be-

4

tween the cages. When they reached the end, Riley pointed to a steel door. "That seems to be how the thief got in," the officer explained.

Using a pocket magnifying glass, Joe examined the scratch marks around the keyhole and along the striker plate. He opened the heavy door and stepped out onto the small cement stoop, checking that side as well.

"So, what do you see?" Price asked Joe from the kennel doorway.

Joe was noncommittal. "As Officer Riley said, this door appears to have been forced open."

"Which cage was the collie in?" Frank asked.

Price gestured toward the cage closest to the steel door. "The cages aren't locked. Too much trouble when it's feeding time."

"That's when I discovered the collie was missing," Iola said. "I did my office work first thing when I got here. That took at least an hour. It wasn't until after I checked to see if the owner had picked up the collie that I knew something was wrong. I called Mr. Price right away."

"And I called the police," Price said.

"Your shift starts at seven, right?" Joe asked Iola.

"Yes, I relieve Dana."

Frank turned to Dana. "Was the collie in his cage when you left?"

"To be honest," Dana said, "I didn't notice. But I didn't hear anything all night. Nobody broke in while *I* was here."

5

"Dana has been with the Doghouse since we opened," Price said. "If she says she didn't hear anything, I believe her."

"Are there any other employees?" Joe asked.

"No," Price replied. "My wife, Nora, and I work the weekends. We've been saving every dime we can for our expansion. We're taking the Doghouse national. I'm telling you, this will be the hottest franchise operation since fast food." Joe glanced around at the many empty cages and raised an eyebrow.

"Business hasn't been all that great yet," Price said defensively, "but just you wait. That's why I can't have any bad publicity."

"There was an animal technician working here when I started," Iola recalled, "and a woman named Maude Macklin. They're both gone."

"That's true," Price said. "We had a young fellow named Mike Trent. We hired him to look after the animals. He came a lot cheaper than a vet, and he was trained to do some of the same things. We haven't replaced either of them yet."

"What happened to Trent?" Frank asked. He jotted down the name in a small notebook.

"I fired him," Price replied. "He refused to hose out the dog runs. He said that wasn't an animal technician's job."

"I knew Mike," Dana Bailey offered. "I'm sure he wouldn't be involved in anything like this."

"What about the Macklin woman?" Frank asked.

6

"She was day manager before me," Iola put in.

"Maude left for a better job," Price said. "She's with that new pet food superstore."

"Can you think of anyone who might hold a grudge against you?" Joe asked.

"Alma Morris," Price said without hesitating. "That woman has tried to stop me from operating the Doghouse since the day its opening was announced in the *Bayport Banner*."

"She lives next door," Dana Bailey explained.

"She's a cat person," Price went on. "There must be a million cats in her house. She hates dogs. The woman circulated a petition trying to prevent the rezoning of this land. When I won the zoning battle, she picketed the construction site. She's written nasty letters to the newspapers. The one they printed last week complained about a so-called dog smell in the neighborhood."

"I don't notice any smell," Frank said. In fact, he noticed, the place looked very clean.

"There have been some phone calls where the person on the other end would hang up as soon as I'd answer," Dana put in. "It could have been the Morris woman. I don't know."

"We'll check it out," Joe said.

"And the collie will turn up," Frank told the group confidently.

"Does this mean you two are going to work on this case?" George Price wanted to know.

"Iola's a close friend," Joe told Price.

7

"Gee," Dana said, "here all this time I've known Iola and she never mentioned she knew you guys."

"Well, standing around talking isn't going to bring the collie back," Price declared. "And I've got work to do." He strode back to the reception area. The others trailed after him.

"And if you'll excuse me," Dana said, "I want to call home and tell my folks where I am." She hurried into the front office and shut the door.

"Did any of those former employees have keys?" Frank asked Price once they were all assembled in the reception area.

"They turned them in. Just as I expect Iola to do." Price held out his hand.

Iola opened her purse. She removed the Doghouse key from her key ring and handed it to Price.

"I can't let the public think I've got a careless staff," he told her.

"The theft was *discovered* while I was on duty," Iola pointed out. "You don't know when the dog was actually stolen."

"There's no evidence that Ms. Morton had anything to do with the theft," Con Riley told Price.

"But I have enough evidence to fire her," Price said coldly. "We were going to have to cover for her anyway, since she was taking time off to go away with her mother."

Price started toward his private office, then stopped. "Oh, and take your dog with you when

8

you leave," he said to Iola, "unless you want to pay the regular daily rate."

"Did you get a dog, Iola?" Joe asked.

"It belongs to Amy Keith," Iola explained as Price went back out to the kennel. "She's on a camping trip. Since I was working here, I told her I'd dog-sit Spike." She hesitated, then looked at Joe with her large brown eyes. "Would you mind watching him while I'm in Boston with Mom?"

"What about your brother?" Frank asked. Chet Morton, Iola's brother, was the Hardys' best friend.

"Didn't he tell you?" Iola asked. "He and Dad are spending some time together—guys only. And," she added before Joe had a chance to suggest it, "Callie's out of town, too." Callie was Frank's girlfriend, and a good friend of Iola.

Joe glanced over at Frank. Frank shrugged.

"Okay," Joe said, sighing. "We'll do it."

Just then Price came back into the lobby leading the oddest-looking dog Frank had ever seen. It was medium-size with huge paws, floppy ears, and a coat that seemed to belong to a long-haired breed on the front end, and a short-haired breed on the back end.

"For some strange reason," Price said sarcastically, "the thief left this fine animal behind."

"Spike might not be a purebred," Iola said hotly, stroking his mottled coat, "but he's a good dog. And he knows more tricks than that collie."

9

Taking a Doghouse brochure from the counter, Iola rolled it up, then held it out. "Spike," she commanded, "Snack!"

Spike leapt high in the air and snatched the rolled-up paper from Iola's hand.

"Good dog," Iola said. She reached into her pocket and pulled out a snack as a reward. "He can sit, roll over, heel, and play dead," she added. Joe knew she wanted them to like the goofy-looking animal.

"Does he eat dog food," Joe said with a smile, "or should we buy him caviar and filet mignon?"

"Very funny," Iola said. Joe's teasing seemed to make her feel a little better.

"As I said, I've got work to do." Price gestured toward the door. "I'm sure you'll keep me informed, officer," he added, looking at Con Riley.

"Of course," Riley said, "but I hope you understand there's no reason to suspect Ms. Morton."

Without another word, Price turned and walked into his office.

Once outside under the portico, Con Riley turned to Frank and Joe. Iola gripped Spike's leash to keep him from chasing a sparrow.

"You know," Riley said, scratching his head, "now that I think about it, there have been a number of dogs reported stolen in Bayport over the past few weeks." He hesitated. "But I can't believe there's any connection between those dogs and this one."

"Why not?" asked Joe.

"They were taken from backyards," Riley explained. "None of them was stolen out of houses or kennels."

"We'd like to see those reports, anyway," Frank told the policeman.

"I can do that," Riley said, "and I hope you'll keep in touch with me, in case you turn up anything that'll help the official investigation."

"Count on it," Frank assured him.

Joe walked Iola to her car as Officer Riley got into his cruiser and drove off in the direction of headquarters.

Frank waited at the van with Spike while Joe wished Iola well on her trip to Boston. When Joe rejoined him, they put Spike in the back, then climbed into the van.

"Let's take Spike home, fix something to eat, then start questioning the suspects," Frank suggested.

Spike stuck his head between the two seats and gave an enthusiastic bark. Joe laughed. "I guess our canine companion approves of your plan, bro, so let's get to it."

Once at the Hardy home, Joe took Spike to a section of the yard next to the garage that was fenced in. Frank got Spike a bowl of water and placed it under a large shade tree.

"We can keep an eye on him from the kitchen," Joe said.

While Joe heated some leftover chicken soup in

the microwave, Frank put generous piles of corned beef, lettuce, and tomatoes on a couple of buns.

Suddenly, from the yard came the sound of a dog barking.

Joe glanced out the window to see if it was Spike. What he saw sent a chill down his spine.

"Frank!" Joe exclaimed. "Someone's grabbed Spike and is taking off with him down the alley. Let's go! Spike's being dognapped!"

2 Off Ramp to Danger

Joe dropped his sandwich on the counter and raced out the kitchen door. Frank was right behind him.

"Did you see which way they went?" Frank asked when he reached the van. Joe was scrambling into the driver's seat.

"They got into a gray car, an old one. I think it had one yellow door."

"It will be much easier to spot if it does," Frank said.

The van spun its rear wheels and lurched backward out of the driveway.

Shifting quickly into gear, Joe raced around the corner of High and Elm Streets and into the alley behind the Hardy home.

13

"There he is," Joe said, "at the end of the alley. He turned right on Sycamore."

The van churned up a cloud of dust as it tore after the dognapper. The gray car was several hundred yards ahead of them, but Frank saw Joe was right. The car had a yellow door.

"The owner must have picked up a replacement door at the junkyard," Joe commented.

"Yeah, but that piece of junk's got a car phone," Frank said, pointing to a small antenna on the back window. "Look—he's getting on the highway."

"I see him." Joe zigged, zagged, then swerved to avoid a slow-moving delivery truck. The van roared up the ramp onto the expressway. "We're closing in," he crowed.

The driver of the gray car pulled into the far left lane. The midday traffic was heavy, but Joe kept him in sight. He was only two car lengths ahead.

Then, tires squealing, the car veered off to the right.

"He's heading for that exit," Frank called above the engine's roar.

Joe maneuvered the van skillfully across two lanes and down the off ramp onto Limehouse Street.

Brick warehouses and boarded-up commercial property zipped past the van windows. Joe recognized Bayport's decaying waterfront district. The area was known for its loud nightclubs and high crime rate.

Joe slowed the van to a reasonable speed. "Which way did he go?" he asked his brother.

"He turned right a couple of blocks down."

Just then Joe heard a siren. Glancing in the rearview mirror, he saw an emergency vehicle gaining on him from behind. Joe knew the law required him to get out of its way.

"They're coming up fast," Frank told his brother. "You'd better pull over."

Joe slammed the heel of his hand on the steering wheel in frustration as the yellow-doored car disappeared up ahead. With the siren practically on top of them, Joe pulled over to the curb and stopped.

The emergency siren screamed past.

"Did we lose him?" Joe asked.

"I think he pulled into a building up ahead. The one by the hydrant."

Joe roared up the street. He slowed outside a dilapidated warehouse. "It looks abandoned," he said.

"Just like the rest of the neighborhood," Frank said. He watched as a homeless man, pushing a grocery cart with a broken wheel, passed by.

Frank noticed that the front of the building had a metal door that rolled up and down on tracks. It was standing wide open.

"I'll bet he's inside," Frank said. "I don't see his car, but he could be waiting back in the shadows."

"Let's park," Joe suggested, "then sneak up on foot." He cruised past the warehouse and pulled

15

over to the curb. "I don't see anyone in the windows," Joe said, scanning the warehouse.

He closed the van door quietly, then stepped across the sidewalk and flattened himself against the wall a foot or so from the open door.

Frank got out of the passenger side of the van, then strode purposefully past the door of the warehouse. He hoped that anyone inside would think he was just another pedestrian walking down the street. He joined Joe just past the doorway.

Joe looked up at a faded Bayport Storage sign bolted to the wall beneath a window. Most of the panes of glass in the window were broken.

"I don't hear a sound," Joe whispered.

Sneaking a peek inside, Joe saw tire tracks in the dust on the floor. He held a finger to his lips, signaling Frank to be quiet. Joe paused, then sprang into the open doorway and looked both ways.

"All clear," he called to Frank. Joe moved on into the building. The warehouse was huge, perhaps a hundred and fifty feet deep. The cement floor was cracked and dusty. Beams of light came through the few grimy windowpanes that weren't cracked or broken. The storage area appeared to turn to the left about halfway into the building. Joe was still too far away to be able to see around the corner.

Frank caught up with Joe. He'd been drawing the tire tread pattern in his notebook. "The tracks turn to the left up ahead," Frank said.

16

"We'd better be careful," Joe cautioned. "He's had time to set up an ambush."

In case the dog thief was listening, Frank pointed silently to the far side of the room. Joe nodded, then cut diagonally across the warehouse until he was against the right wall. He began moving closer to the corner of the L. At the same time, Frank edged forward along the left wall.

Suddenly Frank stopped in his tracks. He'd heard something. It sounded like scratching. Was it an animal? he wondered. Could it be Spike?

When Frank halted, Joe stopped as well. He had heard the same sound. They exchanged a look.

Frank counted to ten. Nothing. No more scratching sound. He raised his hands in a partial karate stance, then he leaped around the corner.

Joe rushed forward to give his brother backup.

The bright sunlight streaming in from another open garage door momentarily blinded Frank. When his eyes adjusted, he saw there was no gray car. And there was no sign of Spike, either. The rest of the area was empty. Dusty tire tracks on the warehouse floor told the story. The dognapper had driven in one door and out the other.

"Obviously, he knows the neighborhood," Joe said, "and he's familiar with this warehouse. He knew he could just cruise on through. We should find out who owns this place."

"Here's something interesting," said Frank. He

17

bent over to pick up a shiny object that caught his eye. He held up a small S-shaped hook.

"What do you think?" he asked Joe.

"It looks like one of those hooks they use to attach licenses to dog collars," Joe replied.

Frank nodded. "It doesn't prove a dognapper was here," said Frank, "but it sure means he could have been." He slipped the tiny piece of metal into his jeans pocket. "What about that scratching sound we heard?" he asked.

"It could have been rats," Joe said.

"Maybe not," Frank said. He pointed to an office just inside the far door. Years before, the word *Manager* had been painted on the now-scuffed surface of the door.

"I'll search the office," Frank told Joe. "You see if you can determine which way the car went."

While Joe followed the tire tracks, Frank walked over to the office. It was dark inside. The windows were blocked by old-fashioned wooden blinds.

Frank tried the doorknob. The office wasn't locked. Inside, something growled.

"Spike?" Frank said.

The growling stopped.

Frank turned the knob. The door creaked on its rusty hinges.

"Spike!" he said again. "That you, fella?"

"Better be careful," Joe called as he made his way back into the warehouse from the street. "Spike doesn't seem like the growling type."

18

Frank pushed the door open and reached around the wall for a light switch. Just as quickly it occurred to him that the electricity had probably been off for years. He brushed against a dusty office chair. Then he heard it again, a low, snarling growl from somewhere across the room.

Frank peered into the darkness.

A compactly built, muscular dog trotted out of the shadows. Frank stopped. He stared transfixed at the dog's electric yellow eyes. It growled menacingly. In the dim light from the open office door, Frank recognized the dog's breed and knew it wasn't Spike.

It was a pit bull.

Suddenly the dog lunged. Frank tried to back out of the way, but he bumped into a broken chair. He raised his arm too late to fend off the dog's glistening fangs. In an instant Frank calculated the dog's target. It was going straight for his throat.

3 The Cats versus the Dogs

Frank snapped his head back just in time. The pit bull missed his throat, but Frank felt the dog's flanks brush roughly across his arm. He had to stop the vicious beast.

Frank saw the dog was wearing a heavy chain collar. When the dog regained its footing and lunged again, Frank ducked to the side at the last moment and grabbed the chromed steel around its neck. The dog jerked to a stop. It yelped in rage and struggled to bend its head around, snapping all the time at Frank.

Frank gripped the chain tight against the back of the dog's neck. Holding the dog as far away from him as he could, he kept its front legs suspended an inch above the floor. The pit bull danced helplessly on its hind legs.

Joe raced into the office. "Don't let go!" he called.

"That's easy for you to say," Frank shot back, raising his voice above the growling and barking of the enraged animal.

Joe spotted a piece of electrical wire in some debris in a corner of the office. The wire was only a few feet long, but it would have to do. Holding on with every ounce of strength he had, Frank gripped the chain while Joe tied one end of the wire through the dog's collar. Together they dragged the snarling dog over to a sturdy-looking standing pipe. Joe looped the wire around the black metal pipe, wrapped it around itself several times, then leaped back.

"Let's hope this holds," Frank said. The wire twanged like a guitar string when the pit bull lunged again, but it held. Panting, the dog glared at Frank. Finally, it sat down.

"Did he get you?" asked Joe.

"No, I'm fine," Frank told him.

"We'll have to call the Humane Society," said Joe. "I wouldn't be surprised if he's one of the stolen animals."

"He's such a warm and cuddly puppy," Frank said sarcastically. "No wonder someone wanted to steal him."

"But how would they steal him?" Joe asked. "I wouldn't touch him with welder's gloves."

Frank looked around the office. Some yellowing papers and candy wrappers were strewn around, but not much else. "There's no sign this pup's been here very long," he said. "He looks well fed, but there's no food or water."

"I'd say the same punk who stole Spike dropped off this guy," Joe concluded. "He would have had time while we were waiting for that emergency squad to pass."

Frank raised the blinds to bring some light into the office. Keeping a distance from the still-growling pit bull, Joe picked through the debris while Frank went through the desk. Except for a few paper clips and some old supply forms, the desk was empty. "Nothing here," Frank told his brother. "Could you tell which way the gray car went?"

"According to the dusty tracks, the driver turned right," Joe said. "But once the car reached the street, the tracks disappear."

"We can drive in that direction when we leave here," Frank suggested. "Maybe we'll spot something."

Seeing nothing else of interest in the warehouse, the brothers returned to their van. Frank raised the lid on the center console. He removed a plastic bag and put the S hook into it, then dropped the bag into the console. Next he pulled out the cellular phone they kept in the van and called the Humane Society. Frank told the official about the pit bull and gave him the address. "And be careful," he added.

As Frank talked, Joe cruised the waterfront. There was no sign of the gray car. "What do we tell Iola?" he asked Frank as they headed home. "She'll kill us when she finds out what happened to Spike."

"She won't be happy," Frank agreed. "I hope we can reach her." He pulled out the phone again and called the Morton home. The answering machine clicked on. Not wanting to leave such an upsetting message on the machine, he disconnected the call.

"I don't recall her telling us where they were staying in Boston," said Joe.

"She didn't," Frank said. "The bad news will just have to wait." He noticed his brother seemed relieved.

Joe parked the van in the garage at the back of the Hardy home. He and Frank could hear the phone ringing as they reached the door.

Joe sprinted inside to answer it. Dana Bailey was calling, and she was still at the Doghouse Pet Motel.

"I just wanted to tell you how sorry I am about Iola," Dana said. "I think she got a bum deal."

"I agree. She didn't deserve to be fired," Joe said. "She's a strong person, though. She'll bounce back quickly."

"Have you had any luck finding the collie?" Dana wanted to know.

"We've got a couple of leads," Joe replied.

"I sure hope you find him," Dana said. "Mr. Price has been impossible ever since it happened. You'd think it was his own dog that got stolen."

"I know how he feels," Joe said. "Someone took Spike right out of our backyard."

"You mean the dog Iola was taking care of?" asked Dana.

"Yeah."

"That's awful," she said. "Do you know who did it?"

"No, but we're going to find out."

"Did you call the police?" Dana asked.

"Not yet. They're already working on finding the stolen collie," Joe explained. "If all of these dog thefts are connected in some way, I imagine they'll find Spike, too."

"I guess that's true," Dana said, then she added, "Oops, there's a customer. I've got to go. Remember, if there's anything I can do to help, just let me know."

Joe thanked her for her concern. "We'll probably stop by the Doghouse sometime tomorrow."

After Joe relayed his conversation with Dana to Frank, Frank nodded and said there wasn't anything more they could do today.

"Let's get something to eat," he said, "then start out early tomorrow. I particularly want to talk to that cat lady."

* * *

24

When Frank entered the kitchen the next morning, Joe was already toasting bagels. "You're up early," the older Hardy commented.

Joe picked up his car keys from the counter. "Let's roll," he said. "We can eat these bagels in the van. I want to nail that dog thief before lunch."

Frank chuckled at his brother's enthusiasm. He clapped a hand on Joe's shoulder as they headed for the van. "You'd rather tangle with a dognapper than tell Iola that Spike was stolen, huh, bro?"

Joe smiled sheepishly. "You got that right." He climbed into the driver's seat and buckled up. Frank did the same.

"Let's question Alma Morris first," Joe suggested as he turned the van onto High Street. "Price's stories about her trying to stop the kennel from being built makes her a prime suspect."

Alma Morris's house, Joe noticed, was the only private home left on the block. All the other buildings had gone commercial. The house was separated from the Doghouse Pet Motel by an overgrown lot. Joe parked in front of the motel, then turned off the engine and studied the Morris residence. It was a small, two-story frame house. All of the shades were pulled down. At the back of the lot was a garage. Joe could see that the windows had been painted over.

"You go talk to the cat lady, and I'll check out that garage," Joe said.

Frank nodded and got out of the van. He walked

up to the low, chain link fence. The gate was unlocked.

Frank rang the doorbell twice before he got a response. The front door, still chained, opened, and a red-haired woman peered at him through the narrow space.

"Alma Morris?" Frank asked.

"Who wants to know?" she demanded.

Frank introduced himself. "I'd like to ask Ms. Morris a few questions about a theft at the Doghouse." he explained.

"I'm Alma Morris, and I don't know anything about it," the woman told him. "But I suppose if I don't talk to you now, you'll never leave me alone." She unchained the door and invited Frank inside.

Alma Morris was much younger than Frank had expected. He'd pictured an eccentric old lady with dyed blue hair pulled back in a bun. Alma Morris had long, auburn hair and didn't appear to be much over thirty. Her white T-shirt said, I Love My Cat.

Alma's youth was only part of the surprise Frank got when he entered the living room. There were countless ceramic cats on the windowsills and bookcases. And every picture hanging on the walls featured at least one feline. But what really threw Frank were the live cats. He had never seen so many cats in one room in his entire life. They were everywhere—sitting on the backs of the couch and the chairs, on the dining room table, running in and out of the kitchen door at the back of the dining room.

"Have a seat," Alma told him, "anywhere that isn't already taken."

"That's easier said than done," Frank pointed out. There was an armchair and hassock across from the couch where Alma sat down. Three cats already occupied the chair. Frank took the hassock.

"Let me guess," Frank said. "You like cats."

"They're nature's perfect animal," Alma Morris declared.

"All these are yours?" Frank asked, gesturing around the room.

"No one ever really owns a cat," Alma replied. "They only make their home here, such as it is, since that vile man opened that dog place."

"Did you know about the collie being stolen from the Doghouse?" Frank asked.

"Of course not," Alma said firmly. "If it's not on the cable news channel, I don't know anything about it. But I'll tell you, if it puts that stupid kennel out of business, that's fine with me."

"Did you know George Price before he opened the Doghouse?" Frank asked. "I was told you tried very hard to stop the Doghouse from opening."

"I'd never heard of George Price until I found out he was plotting to ruin the neighborhood," she said. "You're right I tried to stop him. And I'm not done yet! That kennel smells to high heaven, and when those dogs start barking, my poor kittens can't sleep."

It looked to Frank as though many of the cats were napping quite comfortably just then. And the only smell he detected came from the trays of kitty litter he could see out in the kitchen.

Frank looked around the living room and noticed several pictures on the mantel. He was a little surprised to see they weren't portraits of cats but photographs of people.

"Family pictures?" Frank asked, pointing at the mantel.

"Yes. I don't see most of my relatives anymore because they've moved all over the country. Except for Shawn." She pointed to a photograph of a young man with long hair. "Shawn Cabot. He's my kid brother. Half brother, actually. He's living here, working down at the waterfront."

"He unloads freighters?" Frank prodded.

"No, he's at the dry dock. They're refitting a cruise ship."

"How does he feel about the Doghouse?" asked Frank.

"Just the way I do," Alma said. Then she glared at Frank. "Hey! You're not pinning that theft on Shawn—or on me, either."

"I'm not here to pin anything on anyone," Frank assured her. "But I do have another question. The Doghouse has gotten some odd phone calls lately—"

Alma interrupted Frank before he could finish. "Anything I've got to say to George Price," she said, "I'll say right to his face. Got that? Now, I think we've talked long enough." Alma stood up.

While Frank was with Alma Morris, Joe was trying to see into the garage windows. Whoever had painted them over had done a very thorough job, he thought. He couldn't see a thing. He wondered if Alma had something to hide in there.

Joe spotted a door at the side of the garage. He walked over to it and tried the doorknob. It was locked. He thought that if Spike and the collie were inside, it wouldn't take much to start them barking. He rattled the knob but didn't hear any barking dogs. He leaned close to the door to make sure.

He did hear something else, though, from down the block. Joe recognized the sound. It was the sound of a car door being opened. But not just any door. Someone was opening their van.

Joe figured that his brother had finished talking with Alma and was back at the van. He slipped out of Alma's backyard and sprinted toward the sidewalk.

The passenger door of the van was open. Joe saw someone moving about inside. He didn't recognize the person, but he knew one thing: It wasn't Frank.

4 Who Was That Masked Man?

Joe raced to the van, determined to catch the person in the act. The intruder was hunched over, searching through the glove compartment.

"What do you think you're doing?" Joe demanded when he reached the van. He stood in the open door, blocking any easy escape. The person jerked upright, and his head spun around. Joe's eyes widened. The intruder was wearing a woolen cap. That was odd enough, considering it was summer. But the person was also wearing a rubber mask, making him look doubly strange.

Without responding, the intruder scooped up some magazines that had been sitting on the van floor and flung them directly at Joe's face.

Instinctively, Joe raised his arms and took a step

backward. The hesitation gave the stranger an opening. He slid across into the driver's seat, quickly opened the door, and jumped out the other side.

Joe recovered quickly. He raced around the front of the van and gave chase. But the masked intruder had ducked into the high shrubs, and Joe lost sight of him.

When Joe heard the unmistakable sound of a car starting up, he knew he had lost the guy. Joe jogged back to the van. His brother was standing beside it.

"What happened?" Frank called as Joe approached.

"Someone was going through the van," Joe replied. "He got away. He had a car parked on the other side of those trees."

"Don't worry about it," Frank said. "We'll catch him next time." The brothers climbed into the van, and Frank released the parking brake. "Would you recognize him if you saw him again?"

"Sure, if he's still dressed as the guy from those Fright Night movies," Joe said. He told his brother about the unusual disguise.

"What was he doing?" Frank asked. "Do you think he was trying to steal the van?"

"I think he was looking for something," Joe said. "He was going through the glove compartment when I sneaked up on him." Joe did a quick check of the glove compartment's contents. "The maps are still here, and the warranty book."

"What about the console?" Frank asked.

Joe raised the console lid and studied the contents. "It's gone," he said, irritation in his voice. He rummaged through again. "That hook from the warehouse. He must have taken it."

"It's my fault," Frank said. "I put it in there yesterday, and I should have taken it into the house. Did he get anything else?"

"I don't think so. I'm glad we took the phone inside for the night."

"Hmm. I guess that hook was actually a clue. Obviously, we're onto something." Frank checked the rearview mirror and pulled out into the street. "How about getting some lunch?" he asked. "I saw a diner down at the waterfront yesterday. After lunch we can look up Morris's younger brother."

Frank drove the van down to Limehouse Street. The diner's neon sign said Qui k Lunch. The *c* was burned out.

The brothers took the last booth available in the crowded restaurant, next to the kitchen door.

"What'll it be?" the server asked. Frank learned from her tag that her name was Julie.

"I'll have the hamburger basket and a soda," Frank said.

Joe told Julie to make that two. "Now," he asked Frank, "what's the story with Alma Morris?"

Frank told Joe about Morris's bitter feelings toward George Price and the Doghouse. He added that Morris's half brother was living at her house.

"The guy searching the van could have been Shawn Cabot," Frank said. "If he wasn't at work, he could've seen us parked near his sister's place."

Joe told Frank about his search of Morris's yard. "The garage was locked, and I couldn't see in," he said, "but I'm convinced the dogs aren't there."

When Julie returned with their sodas, Joe asked her if she'd worked long at the diner.

"Too long," she said. "My plans called for me to be a world-famous model two years ago. I'm a little behind schedule."

"I know what you mean," Joe said. "Flash Gordon over here," he said, gesturing toward Frank, "was supposed to pilot the next space shuttle."

Julie laughed. "We don't get many astronauts in here."

"How about guys who drive gray cars with one yellow door?" asked Joe.

"I've seen that car," Julie said. "It's gone by here any number of times. A real heap of junk."

"What about the driver?" Frank asked. "Did you see who was driving?"

"A guy about your age," she said. "But I wouldn't know him if he walked through the door."

"Would you remember the last time you saw the car?" asked Joe.

She thought about it for a minute. "Yesterday, maybe," she said finally.

"There's an empty warehouse just down the

street," Frank said. "Have you noticed any activity around there? People hanging around, cars driving in or out?"

"No. I park near it sometimes, but I've never seen anyone inside."

"Are the doors usually open?" Joe asked.

"Yeah, I think so," Julie said.

A bell on the shelf between the counter and the kitchen rang. "Your burgers are ready," said Julie. "I'd better get them while they're hot."

Joe was hungry. His hamburger was half gone while Frank was still piling up the onions, pickles, lettuce, and tomatoes on his.

"Why are you guys so interested in that car?" Julie wanted to know when she came over to ask if everything was okay. "The driver owe you money?"

"We think he's got a dog we're interested in," Joe told her.

"If you get a dog," Julie said, "you'd better keep an eye on it. I heard there's someone stealing dogs around Bayport. I can't understand why anyone would want to do that."

"We've been wondering the same thing," Frank admitted. "Purebreds are worth some money, especially if they're show dogs."

"The ones I've heard about wouldn't win any prizes," Julie said. "They were just plain old mutts." She began to clear the table. "How about some dessert?" she asked.

After scanning the menu, Frank chose the apple

pie, Joe the peach. While Julie was totaling the check, Joe used the pay phone just inside the diner door by the cash register.

He called a contact who worked at the county tax assessor's office. Joe asked him to find out who owned the warehouse. He gave his friend the address, and the fellow said he'd check it out.

Frank left a tip for Julie and was at the register as Joe was getting off the phone.

"Let's walk over to the dry dock from here," Frank suggested.

Joe waved goodbye to Julie and followed his brother out onto the street.

The cruise ship *Star of Barmet* looked taller than a three-story building. The ship had several ramps and gangways leading up from both sides of a massive concrete slip. Joe had to shade his eyes to see the tops of the cranes and booms high above. They spread over the ship's funnels like elm trees over a street in summer.

"There's the foreman's shack," Frank pointed out. It was a movable metal-and-frame building set up at the bow of the ship. Frank led the way through the shipyard's front gate. The area was alive with the sounds of workers and machinery.

The man just inside the gate was wearing a hard hat labeled Foreman. Frank introduced himself and Joe and told the foreman who they were there to see.

"Shawn Cabot?" the foreman repeated. "I'll have

to check." He took down a black loose-leaf note-book from a sagging shelf.

"Don't remember seeing him today," the fore-man said absently, flipping through the pages. When he found the roster, he moved his index finger down the page. "Nope," he said, "he wasn't scheduled today. Sorry."

"We're not making much progress," Frank said to Joe after they left the shack.

"Let's walk around the waterfront," Joe suggested. "Since Julie said she saw the sedan in the neighborhood yesterday, we may get lucky and spot it."

Frank puzzled over the clues as they walked. "We've got a cat person who hates dogs," he said, "but everything she did to stop the Doghouse from being built was legal. And we don't have any proof she had anything to do with the stolen collie."

"Since Shawn Cabot wasn't at work today, he had the opportunity to search our van," Joe pointed out. "He could have heard his sister talking to you and decided to take matters into his own hands."

"It's possible," Frank said. The brothers walked the next few blocks in silence, each mulling over the case.

"Check it out," Frank said, pointing across the street. They had come to the warehouse the dognapper had driven through.

"The overhead door is closed," Joe noted. "Didn't Julie say that the door was usually open?"

Joe waited until a slow-moving red pickup truck passed by, then he jogged across to the sidewalk outside the warehouse. He walked to the end of the building, then around the corner. Both overhead doors, he saw, had been closed and locked.

"Someone decided to put their property in order," Frank said when he reached Joe's side. He pointed out a fresh For Sale sign next to the door.

"Or they want to discourage us from going inside again," Joe said.

They walked over to the Dumpster behind the old building. Frank held up the lightweight plastic cover. "There's a desk in here," Frank said, looking in, "and a chair. It looks like they've cleared out the office. They must have cleaned out the place to put it on the market." He recognized the yellowed newspapers as part of the debris he'd seen in the office the day before.

Frank started to put the Dumpster lid back down when he saw something poking out of the papers. "Hold it open," he instructed Joe. "I want to do some trash-picking." Frank nimbly leaped up and over the side of the Dumpster.

He bent down and picked up the stained newspaper. A small business card fell out. "We missed this yesterday," Frank said. He held up the card for Joe to see.

"'Excelsior Laboratories,'" Joe read aloud. "'Commercial Testing—One Case or Entire Projects.' The address is on the north side of Bayport. Do you think there's any connection?"

"Could be a coincidence," Frank admitted. "It could've been left by someone who used to work at the warehouse. Or the dog thief could have dropped it."

Frank turned the card over. There was a word scrawled on the back " 'Skinner,' " he read. "Who or what is Skinner?" He slipped the card into the pocket of his jeans.

"Beats me," Joe said.

Frank climbed back out of the Dumpster and brushed himself off. "Let's check on the owner of this building. Maybe our friend downtown has the answer."

Frank drove. The courthouse was on the north side of the Bayport town square. Parking spaces were usually hard to find during business hours, but Frank got lucky. He slipped into a spot just as a sports car tried to beat him to it.

"There are a lot of crazy drivers in this world," Frank said, chuckling. He set the brake and took the keys out of the ignition.

"I hope my friend has the information ready," Joe said, opening the passenger door.

Frank took a quick look in the rearview mirror before opening his door. Traffic was surprisingly light for midday. All Frank saw was a faded red pickup truck turning onto the street. Frank got out and was locking the van when he heard the sound of a vehicle suddenly accelerating.

Frank looked up and saw that the truck was picking up speed as it angled away from the middle of the street.

It was headed toward the Hardys' van.

"What's that guy think he's doing?" Frank called over to Joe. "Playing chicken?"

"I don't think he's playing," Joe said, getting out onto the sidewalk.

"I think you're right," Frank said. He started around the front of the van, but saw he'd waited too long. He was caught between the van and the car parked in front of it when the truck hit.

Frank heard the echoing thump as the truck's right front fender smacked the back of the van. Frank heard the squawking sound caused by the van's parking brake being severely stressed. More ominously, he felt the van's bumper push against his lower leg. He knew with sickening clarity what was going to happen next. He was about to be crushed.

5 Hit-and-Run

Frank moved quickly. Putting his left hand on the trunk lid of the car parked in front of him, and his right on the van's grillwork, he hoisted himself up like a gymnast on parallel bars. His toes just cleared the van's bumper as the two vehicles banged together.

From the sidewalk, Joe saw what was happening. He raced to the front of the van.

"Jump over!" he called to Frank. "I'll catch you."

Frank didn't have to be told twice. In a continuation of the same motion that allowed his feet to clear the colliding cars, he swung forward. Joe grabbed him around the waist, breaking his fall.

The red truck scraped along the side of the van and roared past. Frank tested his foot. He had come down hard, but luckily he hadn't twisted or sprained anything.

"Whoever that was," Joe commented, "he was aiming right at us."

"I didn't notice the truck until the last moment," Frank said, disgusted with himself. "And I sure didn't catch the license number."

"He left some paint on the van," Joe said. He studied it for a moment. "You know, there was a truck like that down at the waterfront. I waited for it to pass when we crossed the street to the warehouse."

"I remember," said Frank. "He was going a lot more slowly then."

"Maybe because he was watching us," Joe concluded. "He must have followed the van here."

Frank scanned the town square. "He's gone now. Let's go on over to the courthouse." He looked in both directions, then led the way across the square.

Joe told the receptionist in the tax office who he was and whom he and Frank wanted to see. The receptionist said they were expected and handed Joe a note.

"'Sorry I can't see you. I'm in a meeting. The county's replacing old computers with a new system,'" Joe read to Frank. "'Still not up and running but expect to be on-line later today. I haven't forgotten. Keep in touch.'"

"We told Dana we might stop by and talk to her again," Frank said as the brothers walked back across the green. "Let's see if she's over at the Doghouse."

Frank used the phone in the car. George Price's wife, Nora, answered. She told Frank that Dana had the afternoon off. "We need her for the night shift," Nora Price explained.

"Has there been any more trouble?" asked Frank.

"Not a bit," she said. "I think the theft was an isolated incident. I can give you Dana's number at her apartment. She seems to be out a lot, but she's got an answering machine."

Frank wrote down the number. Then he thanked Price, hung up, and punched in Dana's number.

"Dana," Frank said when she answered. "It's Frank Hardy. We wondered if we could talk to you. How about if we stop by?"

"No, no, my apartment's a mess," Dana said, "but I can meet you somewhere."

When Frank told her they were in downtown Bayport, Dana assured them she could be there in fifteen minutes.

A short time later, Joe saw Dana get off the bus on the other side of the park.

"My car's in the shop," she explained.

Frank bought three bottles of soda and large pretzels from a street vendor, and the three sat down on one of the park benches. Tall oak trees shielded them from the hot afternoon sun.

"So how's it going?" Dana asked after a bite of her pretzel.

"George Price seems to think Alma Morris is the culprit in this mystery," Frank said. "Has Ms. Morris ever done anything threatening while you've been at work?"

"There have been those weird hang-up calls," said Dana, "but I can't prove it was Morris."

"What about her younger brother?" asked Frank. "His name is Shawn Cabot."

Dana rolled her eyes. "I know Shawn," she said. "He asked me out, but I couldn't go. The night shift is murder on your social life. And do you know what that guy said? He told me after the Doghouse is closed down, I'll have plenty of time to see him."

"This woman who worked at the Doghouse when it opened," Frank said. "Maude Macklin. We understand she quit because she got a better job."

"That's not exactly how it happened," Dana said. "She quit when Mr. Price gave the big management job to his wife instead of her. I don't know why Maude was so surprised. That sort of thing happens all the time."

"Did she ever threaten the Prices?" asked Joe. "Or the Doghouse?"

"She made all kinds of crazy threats," said Dana. "She was screaming about how she had the training but the boss's wife had the connections. She threw some dog bowls on the floor. I remember she said she didn't care if she knocked down the whole building. Maude was really steamed."

43

"Have you talked to her since she left the Doghouse?" asked Frank.

"A few times," Dana replied. "I called her at her new job, just to see how she was doing."

"So Macklin's working at a pet store now?" Joe asked Dana.

"She's running Pet Provisions. It's that new building across from the Bayport Mall."

"What about the other employee?" Frank asked. "The one who was fired."

Dana glanced at her watch. "Mike Trent?" She shrugged her shoulders. "I haven't heard anything about him. Listen," she continued, "I've got to get going. If you talk to Maude, tell her I said hello."

Joe asked Dana if they could give her a lift. She thanked them but said she had an appointment.

Frank told her other questions might come up.

"No problem," Dana said with a smile and a wave.

As Frank drove up to Pet Provisions he saw that the supermarket-size pet food store was at the back of a crowded parking lot.

" 'Where America's Pets Love to Shop,' " Frank read from the huge banner across the front of Pet Provisions.

"Hurry up and park," Joe said. "I can't wait to see the hamsters pushing shopping carts around."

Inside, a harried store clerk pointed out Maude Macklin. The young woman, who appeared to be in her twenties, was stationed at the first register. Frank guessed she was a hands-on kind of manager. Why else would she be bagging her customers' purchases? She reached down and patted an Irish setter straining at its leash. "Stormy's a nice name," she was saying when Frank and Joe walked up to her.

Frank introduced himself and his brother.

"We'd like to ask you some questions about the Doghouse," Joe informed her.

Maude's smile faded quickly. She excused herself, telling the checkout person she'd be in her office. She led the brothers past rows of pet supplies to the back of the store. Frank noticed that the store was organized by pet type. Dogs had their own section, then cats. There were tropical fish tanks and bird cages. The sounds of parrots and barking dogs filled the large store.

"There are your hamsters," Frank said as they passed. "But I don't see any shopping carts."

Maude Macklin shot them a puzzled look. "I saw the article in the *Banner* about the missing dog," she said as she dodged around a forklift with yellow and black warning stripes and headed to the back of the store. Her office was one of several rooms in the vast storage area behind the selling floor. "Please sit down," she told the Hardys.

"We understand you and George Price didn't part company on friendly terms," Frank said.

"It was no big deal," Macklin replied. "He'd led me to believe I'd be the new district manager when he opened his chain of dog motels. Apparently he changed his mind because he gave the job to his wife."

"You were overheard making threats against him and his place of business," said Joe.

"Look, I was upset," she said. "I don't know what you heard, but I sure didn't threaten to steal any dogs." She leaned forward and glared at Joe. "George Price lied to me," Macklin said sharply. "I thought we had an understanding. He reneged."

"You're a manager here," said Frank. "Isn't this a better job?"

"I'm an *assistant* manager," Macklin said. Frank heard no trace of pride in her voice. Obviously Macklin didn't see her job at Pet Provisions as a step up. "It's just a fancy title for a lot of thankless jobs. You saw me out there working the line. After hours I help unload the trucks."

"You sell animals here as well as supplies," Frank commented. "The dog stolen from the kennel was a collie, a valuable show dog."

"Puppies!" she exclaimed. "We sell puppies. We get them from well-known breeders and keep very detailed files."

The filing cabinets behind Macklin's desk were clearly labeled. The one that interested Frank read Purebreds. A quick glance at the files on Macklin's

46

desk revealed a folder with the label Canine Adoptions.

Frank looked up at Maude and saw that she'd been watching him. "If you think there are any stolen dogs around here," she said, "go ahead and search all you want." She placed a glossy cat magazine over the folder on her desk. "My business files are off-limits," she said firmly.

Frank gave her a questioning look.

"My sales are confidential," Macklin went on, "but Mike Trent can show you around when he gets here. I'm too busy."

"Mike Trent is working here?" asked Joe. "The same Mike Trent from the Doghouse?"

"What if it is?" Macklin was clearly getting irritated.

"No one's accusing you of anything," Frank said, backing off slightly, "but it raises a question when two people who were angry when they left the Doghouse are working together at new jobs."

"I resent your implication," Macklin said. "If you don't mind, I've got work to do."

"We'd like to talk to Mike," said Frank.

"He's out on a delivery," she said curtly.

"When will he be back?" asked Joe.

"I have no idea." Macklin got up from behind her desk. "Now, if you'll excuse me." She walked over to the office door.

"Thanks for your cooperation," Joe said dryly.

The door slammed behind them.

"Maybe she'd be more friendly if we bought a couple of bags of chow," Joe joked. He waved a hand at the thousands of pounds of pet food filling the storeroom. The kibble was in twenty-pound bags, stacked on wooden skids. The neat rows were a full ten feet high.

Frank was immediately aware of work noises in the vast warehouse. He heard what sounded like a heavy pallet hit the concrete floor. Moments later the forklift used for moving the pallets zipped past an intersection at the end of the aisle where he and Joe were walking. The humming of the small truck's electric motor grew louder. It sounded to Frank as if the forklift turned into the lane next to theirs.

Joe was several steps ahead of Frank. He was about to comment on the number of brands when he heard a loud thump. Suddenly the wall of dog food next to him began moving. One of the skids was being pushed into the lane in front of Joe.

"Hey," Joe called. "People coming through over here!"

The stack continued moving.

Joe looked up just in time to see the stack of bags waver. Instinctively, he threw his arms over his head. It was a futile gesture. The pile started to topple. So did the one next to it.

As he turned to warn Frank, the first of the bags struck Joe on the head. The next two staggered him. He tried to keep his balance, but it was impossible. The entire pile was collapsing. Joe was being crushed by thousands of pounds of dog food.

6 Kibbled to Bits

A ton of kibble cascaded down on top of Joe. Seconds later Frank himself was knocked to the floor by a pallet of pet chow. When he tried to back away, a bag struck him on the head, stunning him for a second. More bags piled up around him.

When the avalanche ended, Frank struggled to his feet and looked around for his brother. Joe had been only steps in front of him. Was he buried under that mountain of kibble?

Frank had to hurry. The pile was as tall as he was. If he didn't rescue his brother fast, Joe could suffocate.

Frantically, the older Hardy began pulling the heavy bags away from the center of the aisle. It seemed to take forever. Finally Frank heard a groan. After removing several more bags, he saw Joe's shoulder and arm.

"Joe? Can you hear me?" he called frantically. Frank shoved a few more bags aside until he could see Joe's face.

"This kibble sure is a heavy diet." Joe managed a weak smile.

Frank eased off the last of the bags and helped his brother to his feet.

"You all right?" Frank asked.

"I'll live," Joe said, brushing the dust from his jeans.

Frank scrambled over the rest of the fallen dog food and ran across to the next aisle. The forklift was parked, with no one around.

Rejoining Joe, Frank signaled his brother to follow him. They marched back to Maude Macklin's office. Joe flung the door open, and he and Frank stepped inside.

Maude looked up from the paperwork on her desk. "What do you think you're doing?" she demanded.

"Someone just tried to kill us," Joe said.

"Well, it wasn't me," Maude said. Frank and Joe insisted she accompany them to the scene of the "accident." Macklin surveyed the mess.

"You guys are being too dramatic," she said. "The bags were just stacked too high."

"How many clerks do you have on the sales floor?" Joe asked.

"Six," Maude said. "Check them out if you want. I'll be in my office." She turned, then stopped.

"You were looking for Mike Trent," Macklin said. "There he is." She pointed through one of the large plate glass windows.

Joe followed her gaze. A young man with long dark hair was getting out of a Pet Provisions company van.

"Let's talk to him outside," Frank suggested. He stepped into the automatic door's electronic field, and the brothers headed out to the parking lot.

"Mike Trent!" Joe called. The young man was locking the van.

"Yeah?" Trent stopped and turned around.

"We were told you used to work at the Doghouse Pet Motel," Frank said. He introduced himself and Joe.

"You were told right," Trent replied.

"Why'd you leave that job?" Frank asked.

"I didn't like the duties Price was giving me," Trent said. "I'm a registered animal technician. That means I can work with a veterinarian. It's sort of like being a nurse to animals. I wasn't going to hose out the cages."

"And you've been working here since?" Joe asked Trent.

"Maybe it doesn't look like much," Trent said defensively, "but at least Maude's been straight with me. And she gives me real responsibility."

52

"What do you mean?" asked Frank.

"She lets me set up the animals' diets and their feeding schedules."

Joe asked, "You didn't do those things at the Doghouse?"

"Why are you asking me all of these questions?" Trent wanted to know.

"A valuable dog was stolen from the kennel," said Joe.

"No way!" Trent exclaimed. It seemed to take a moment for the significance of the Hardys' presence to sink in. "Wait a minute," he said suddenly. "I hope you don't think I know anything about it."

"We've heard a lot of different stories and we wanted to check them out. Did you ever have keys to the Doghouse?" Frank asked.

"Just while I was on duty," Trent said, "but I turned them in when I left."

"Maude Macklin told us you were making a delivery," Frank said. "Is that something animal technicians normally do?"

Trent laughed. "No, not usually, but she's trying to work her way up to manager, and she needed me to pitch in. Her success is my success."

"One more thing before we go," Frank said. "Did you just get back to the store?"

"Sure," Trent replied. "Why?"

"Just wondered," Joe said. He thanked Trent for his trouble. "We'll stay in touch," he added.

"Did you notice anything unusual in Maude Macklin's office?" Joe asked Frank as Frank steered their van out of the Pet Provisions lot.

"I give up," Frank said.

"Large pet carriers. She had several of them in her office."

"They sell pet carriers," Frank said. "I saw an entire section of them, some big enough for a Saint Bernard."

"The ones in Macklin's office are used. And one of them is big enough for a collie."

"She said they sell puppies," Frank said thoughtfully, "so why would she have several used grown-dog-size carriers? What grown dogs have they been carrying? And I wonder why she made such a point about her office files," he added. "What's in those files she doesn't want us to see?"

"Let's find out," Joe said, "tonight. We'll get some supper. Then, after the place has closed, we'll pay a second visit to Pet Provisions. One of those files may contain a bill of sale for a collie."

That night Joe parked the van across from the pet supermarket.

"Let's circle around behind," Joe said. "And keep to the shadows."

"How do we get in?" Frank whispered when they'd reached the back of the building. There was a single roadway running along a deep ravine.

"Right up there," Joe said. He pointed out a window that was open a crack. "Boost me up."

Frank made a foothold with his hands. Joe stepped up, then sprang upward as Frank lifted. Joe managed to hook his fingers over the aluminum window frame. The sharp frame dug into his fingers, but Joe managed to hold on. With Frank still hoisting, Joe got high enough to slide the window open with his other hand. Then, with a final effort, he flopped over the sill.

After making sure that the storeroom didn't have a security system, Joe unlatched the back door and admitted his brother.

Frank clicked on his pocket flashlight, and the two brothers made their way to the selling floor.

Frank noticed that the fallen piles of dog chow had been restacked. He wondered if Mike Trent was the one who had had to straighten up the mess. He also wondered if it had been Mike Trent who had knocked them over.

"Let's split up," Joe suggested. He turned toward Maude Macklin's office. "I'll check out those files," he told Frank.

Frank nodded agreement and moved off to another part of the storeroom.

Joe switched on his flashlight. Macklin's desk was messy, but it didn't look much different from when he and Frank were there earlier.

He began looking through Macklin's papers: invoices, advertisements, dummied layouts for up-coming ads. The bottom drawer on the right side of the desk contained a number of job applications. One of them was Mike Trent's. Joe scanned it quickly.

In another part of the storeroom, Frank was examining the forklift. The thing probably had fingerprints all over it, he figured, but it had been moved since the stacks were pushed over. In any case, he knew it wouldn't prove a thing if prints belonging to the people who worked at Pet Provisions showed up on it.

Suddenly Frank switched off his light. He thought he had heard something. Was it Joe? Frank didn't want to risk calling out. He was about to turn the flashlight back on when he heard the noise again. It came from a small room adjacent to Macklin's office.

Frank crept forward. The door, he noticed, was ajar.

He listened. Hearing nothing, he reached out and eased the door open. He switched his flashlight back on and trained it on the interior. It was a supply room. Frank saw cleaning fluids and drums of floor wax. He stepped into the room.

As he entered the room, Frank saw a shadowy form just inside the door. Before he could do anything to defend himself, a mop handle crashed down sharply on his head. Unconscious, Frank slumped to the floor.

Meanwhile, Joe was still sorting through Maude Macklin's files. Aside from Mike Trent's job application, he hadn't found anything of importance to the case. All sales seemed to be of puppies. There was no mention of a collie. He did find a clipping from the *Bayport Banner*. The headline read, "Is Bayport's New Dog Motel in the Doghouse?" The article detailed Alma Morris's many legal maneuvers to stall the opening. It ended with her ringing declaration that she'd close the place down if it was the last thing she ever did.

Why would Macklin save this article? Joe wondered. And how far would Alma Morris go to achieve her goal?

Some handbills caught Joe's eye. Pet Provisions was sponsoring a pet show. Owners were encouraged to bring their pets in carriers. If they didn't have carriers, the store could supply them. That might account for the used carriers, Joe thought.

He started putting things back in place when he heard a sound. Joe was so intent on getting the desk arranged just right that he didn't pay much attention. He figured it was Frank.

The blow to his head was sharp and surprising. As he slumped to the ground he realized the sound he'd heard hadn't been his brother.

57

It seemed like hours had passed when he came to. Joe's head throbbed. He tried to sit up, but his head hit something. He groaned at the fresh pain. Where was he? Why was the ceiling so low?

Slowly his vision cleared, and he was able to see a little better. What he saw was strange. He was looking at tiny metal bars, very close together.

"Where am I?" he muttered, then, "Frank?"

Silence. It was as quiet as a tomb.

Joe's head still hurt, and he was too dizzy to move any more. He was really uncomfortable. His knees were smashed up into his chest. As his eyes adjusted to the darkness, he realized he couldn't stand if he tried. He was in some kind of a large box. The computer-white textured sides were broken by two small barred windows, one on each side. The bars were shiny steel. In front of him was a square barred door. It was chained and padlocked.

Joe looked more closely at his prison. It was just the right size for a German shepherd or a Doberman. Then he understood. He was locked inside a large pet carrier.

7 4B or Not 4B?

Joe yanked on the chain that locked him in his prison. It made a lot of noise, but there was no way Joe could pull it loose from the gate. He was locked in.

"Is that you, Joe?"

It was Frank. He was somewhere very close.

"Where are you?" Joe asked.

"I'm your next-door neighbor," Frank said.

Being careful not to hit his head again, Joe eased over to the barred window and looked out. Frank was peering back at him through a similar window in his own cage.

"Did you see who got you?" Frank asked.

"No," Joe answered. "Whoever it was got me from behind."

"Same here," Frank said. "Someone has been with us every step of the way."

"Why?" Joe asked. "What's the big deal about two stolen dogs? What are they afraid we'll find out?"

"It's not just two dogs. I'm sure it has something to do with the other reports of stolen dogs."

"I saw Mike Trent's job application," Joe told Frank. "He lives down in the waterfront area, not more than a couple of blocks from that warehouse."

"Let's go see him," Frank said, then he added, "as soon we get out of these cages."

"Just how do you propose the getting-out-of-these-cages part?" Joe wanted to know.

Frank studied his prison. He looked across at Joe's pet carrier. The cages had been cast in halves. The two parts were held together by short bolts through a lip on each half of the cage.

"Brute force," Frank said. "These things are plastic, sort of like those new garbage cans." Frank braced himself against one side of the pet carrier. Next he wedged himself sideways and pressed both feet against the window as hard as he could. When it gave a little, he pulled back his feet, then kicked.

He kicked again and again, then pushed hard, groaning with each exertion. The fourth time his foot went right out through the opening. The bars clattered and skidded across the smooth concrete floor.

Wasting no time, Frank reached out. His fingers

60

found the first bolt. The nut was screwed on tight, but after working with it for several minutes, he felt it turn. Seconds later the nut hit the floor.

"Is it working?" called Joe.

"A couple more minutes should do it," said Frank. "Say, why are you just sitting there?"

Joe laughed. "I figured I'd wait and see how you did before I tried to make a break," he explained.

Frank shook his head in exasperation, and instantly regretted it. It started throbbing. Oh, well, he thought, back to work.

The second bolt was easy. The third didn't want to let go, but eventually he worked it loose as well.

Frank knew there had to be a quicker way.

He knelt in his prison, then raised up until his back was up against the top of the carrier. "Stand back," he warned Joe, who was watching through his cell window.

Frank gritted his teeth and pushed. He put most of his force on the side where he'd removed the bolts.

"It's giving," he reported. He caught his breath, then pushed upward again. He could feel the plastic give, then rip loose from the rest of the bolts. "All right!" he said triumphantly.

Frank quickly loosened the bolts on Joe's cage. A minute more and his brother was free.

"This was really embarrassing," Frank complained. "I mean, being locked in dog carriers."

"I won't tell anyone if you won't," Joe assured

him. He looked at his watch. "It's late, but let's drive over to Mike Trent's place."

Joe cruised slowly down Water Street. "The address would be on the left side," he told Frank. "Seventeen eighty-one. It must be that apartment building there." Joe pointed to a run-down building across the street.

"Did you write down the apartment number?" Frank asked.

"It's four-something," he told Frank. "Don't worry, we'll find it."

Joe pulled up to the curb in front of the building. Late as it was, there were still a lot of lights on.

"Maybe his name is on one of the mailboxes," Frank said when they reached the entrance. He scanned the two rows of tiny labels on the mailboxes. Most of them were blank. A few of the names were typed; some were written in pencil.

"There are four apartments on the fourth floor," said Frank, "and none of them says Mike Trent."

"This one says Montrose," said Joe.

"That eliminates Four C."

Frank was looking at the bulletin board next to the mailboxes. "Here's a notice from the landlord," he said. "According to this, apartment Four D has been for rent since February."

"That leaves A and B," Joe said. "Let's just go on up and knock." He turned to start upstairs. The inner door wouldn't open.

"It's got a security system," Joe said. "We'll have to buzz his apartment."

"Excuse me," said an older man who had entered the foyer. He pushed past them and unlocked the door. He stepped inside and started up the stairs.

"I guess we won't," said Frank, catching the inner door before it could latch again.

Frank hoped their footsteps on the stairs wouldn't disturb the tenants, but he needn't have worried. The sounds of televisions and babies crying filled the hallways.

The landing on the fourth floor was dark. The bulb in the overhead fixture had burned out. The apartment for rent had a plastic bag filled with junk mail hanging from the doorknob.

"Four A's awake," Joe said. The bass was turned up so high on the stereo inside that the landing was vibrating.

Frank knocked on the door. When no one responded, he knocked again, much louder.

"Yeah?" someone shouted inside. "What d'ya want?"

Frank looked at Joe, then shouted, "Ace Pest Control. Mr. Trent called us from this address."

"Pest control? At this time of night?" It was a man's voice.

"Bugs never stop," Joe replied, "so neither do we."

"Nobody called from here," the man hollered back.

"Is this Four A?" Frank asked.

The apartment door opened. Frank found himself looking at an unshaven man of perhaps fifty. The man was wearing a stained T-shirt and grubby pants.

"Who'd you say called?" the man asked.

Frank pulled his notebook from his back pocket. "Mike Trent," he said.

"Nobody by that name here," he said.

"We must have written down the wrong apartment number," said Joe. "Maybe he lives across the hall. He's young, about our age, has long brown hair."

"Sounds like the guy," the man said. "But I think he moved out today. Afternoon sometime. I heard all this noise, and when I looked he was carrying boxes down the stairs."

"Is his name Mike Trent?" asked Frank.

"Do I look like the building social director or something?" the man asked. "I don't know what his name is and I don't care."

"Did Mr. Trent have a dog?" Joe asked.

"No dogs allowed in this building," the man snapped.

"How about a roommate?" Frank asked. "Or a girlfriend?"

"I'm not answering any more questions," said the man. "Good night!"

"Sorry we bothered you," Joe told the man as he slammed his apartment door in Joe's face.

"Have a nice day," Frank said sarcastically. He turned and looked at the door across the hall. It was scarred, and the B was hanging by one small nail.

Joe leaned forward, listening. He looked at the crack between the edge of the door and the door-jamb. "It's open," he said.

He gave the door a gentle nudge. It swung open a couple of inches. Joe peered inside.

"See anything?" Frank whispered.

"Looks empty."

Joe put his hand to the door to push it farther open. Suddenly the door swung back in a rush of air. Joe looked up in time to see a shadowy figure standing just inside the apartment. Joe couldn't make out the face under the baseball cap that was pulled low over the person's eyes.

"Mike Trent?"

If it was Trent, he didn't answer. Instead, he pointed a small cylinder at Joe and sprayed. There was a low hissing sound. Joe's hands went to his eyes. Whatever the stuff was, it burned. And it was blinding him.

"Watch out, Frank!" he called. "That guy's—" Joe staggered back out to the hallway.

Frank grabbed Joe by the shoulders at the last moment, catching him before he fell down the stairwell. Out of the corner of his eye, Frank saw the figure coming at him. And then he heard the hiss. The man was spraying him now.

Frank threw his arms up over his eyes. He felt the

chill of the aerosol's propellant. The sensation of wetness spread across his face.

Frank felt the man push him out of the way, then he heard him run down the stairs. Frank rubbed his eyes. He was desperate to wipe the stuff out. It didn't work. When he took his hands away, he couldn't see. Panic began to rise up in him. Had he gone blind?

8 A New Paint Job

"Joe, I can't see!" Frank called out.

"I can't, either," Joe replied. "I think we were sprayed with pepper gas. We've got to wash this stuff out of our eyes before it does any permanent damage."

"I didn't hear the door to the apartment close," Frank said. "Just stay against the wall and work your way around to your left."

"Okay," Joe said. Frank could hear him sliding along the plaster. He made a scuffing sound.

"I'm in," Joe announced. "But I don't have any idea where the kitchen or bathroom is."

"Stay right there and talk me in," Frank said. "I'll help you feel around for a sink."

A few moments later Frank was inside apartment Four B.

"I didn't see any furniture when I looked in," Joe told him. "I'll keep going left. You head right." The Hardys began to grope around the apartment, stumbling occasionally.

"Over here!" Joe finally called. He had reached the kitchen sink and had turned on the water. He was splashing his face furiously.

"The water's working," Joe announced. "I can see."

Frank followed Joe's voice. It wasn't long before the brothers had rinsed the pepper gas out of their eyes.

"Could you tell who it was?" Frank asked Joe.

"I saw a cap, but his face was in the shadows," said Joe. "How about you?"

"I saw only his spray can." Frank sighed disgustedly. "I'm getting tired of these attacks. If all this is being done by one guy, I wish he'd get a life doing something else. I could use the break."

"We'll catch him," Joe said. "But as long as we're here, let's search the place."

Frank took the bedroom and the closets, Joe the living room and kitchen. The tenant hadn't left the place exactly clean, but there wasn't a clue to be found.

"There's nothing here," Frank said finally. "No sign of dogs, and not a single scrap of evidence."

Joe sighed. "Maybe there's something on our

answering machine about the ownership of that warehouse," he said hopefully.

As soon as they got home, Joe hurried to the phone and punched the button. Their friend had called. "The computers still aren't running," his message said, "but when I find out, I'll call you right away."

Disappointed, the Hardys trudged up the stairs, changed quickly, and then fell into their beds, exhausted.

"Remind me to check Dad's fax machine first thing tomorrow," Frank said as he drifted off into a deep sleep.

Joe was in the Hardy kitchen the next morning. He had just cracked some eggs into a frying pan.

When Frank entered the kitchen, he was holding three sheets of police reports, which officer Riley had sent over by fax. "Joe," Frank said, waving the papers, "the dogs were stolen from all over town. It's as if the thief drove around looking for animals to steal. And they're not all pedigreed. A few are valuable, like the collie, but most of them are just mutts."

"So what are you saying?" Joe asked. He slid a couple of eggs onto Frank's plate.

"I'm saying the thief wants dogs. He doesn't care what kind, particularly, just as long as they're dogs."

"Okay," Joe said. "What does he want them for?

Do you think he's got a pet shop somewhere filled with hot dogs?" He laughed at his own joke.

"He wants to sell them all right," said Frank, "but not at any pet shop." Frank handed Joe the business card they'd found in the Dumpster outside the warehouse.

"'Excelsior Labs,'" Joe read aloud. "So?"

"My guess is he's planning to sell the stolen dogs to laboratories for research," Frank said. "That's why it doesn't matter what kind of dogs they are."

"Anyone could have dropped this card," Joe pointed out.

Frank sighed. "I know, but right now it's the only lead we've got."

Joe didn't say anything. He looked at the card, then at his brother. "You could be right," he said. "There are a lot of people against using animals in experiments, but it's still being done. And, of course, there is plenty of research being done, in which the animals' behavior is studied and the animals are not harmed. If the usual sources for lab animals dry up, our thief might just have found himself a way to make some easy money."

"Which means we've got to hurry and catch him before he has a chance to sell them. Spike's life depends upon it."

Frank picked up the phone and called Excelsior Labs. Because it was still early, he wasn't surprised when a machine answered. The recorded message

70

informed him that the lab opened at nine-thirty. He glanced at his watch. It was just nine o'clock.

"While we're waiting, let's call the people whose dogs were stolen and see if any of them can help us," Joe suggested, "then we'll pay a visit to Excelsior Labs."

For the next half hour the brothers made phone calls. Most of the dogs, like Spike, had been stolen from their own yards. A couple had been in runs. One was last seen in its doghouse. Not one of the owners of the stolen dogs had seen any strangers hanging around the neighborhood. Nor had anyone noticed any suspicious cars or trucks in the neighborhood. They were all distressed by the disappearances. "Fluffy is our daughter's best friend," a mother confided in Frank. "I don't know if she'll ever get over losing her puppy."

"We'll do our best to find Fluffy," Frank promised.

"There should be a special punishment for a person who would steal a child's pet," Joe said angrily when he'd made his last call.

Frank glanced at the hall clock. "If we leave now," he said, "the lab ought to be open by the time we get there."

Excelsior Laboratories was located in an industrial park west of Bayport. The one-story white brick building had few windows. It looked as if it could have been an office, a school, or even a small

71

warehouse. A sign said Excelsior, but Frank didn't see the word *laboratory* anywhere.

Frank pulled into the parking lot. He took a spot with Visitor painted between the yellow lines.

The lab's lobby featured a waiting area and a white counter. The receptionist, a young woman in her twenties, was speaking into her headset.

Looking down at the switchboard, Frank spotted a button with the name *Skinner* next to it. That was the name that was written on the back of the business card, he realized.

The receptionist switched off the call. She was asking Frank and Joe if she could help them when a middle-aged man in a white coat swept into the lobby through double doors.

"What can Excelsior Labs do for you fellows?" he asked jovially.

Joe introduced himself, then Frank.

"Dr. Evan Beck," said the man in the lab coat.

"We'd like to speak with Skinner," Frank said. He didn't know if Skinner was a doctor, an administrator, or a technician. He didn't even know if the person was male or female.

"You have an appointment?" asked Dr. Beck.

"No, but we're here on important business." Frank explained their mission to find Spike in the very briefest of terms.

"I guess it's all right," Dr. Beck said. He led the Hardys through the swinging door into the lab's work area. There was a row of offices, then two large laboratories down the hall.

Skinner's office was the first one they came to. When the Hardys and Dr. Beck walked into the office, Joe noticed the title Dr. on the nameplate on the desk.

Dr. Jan Skinner was barely thirty. Her brown hair was held back from her face by barrettes. The dark horn-rimmed glasses gave her a scholarly look.

Frank took care of the introductions. "Does this lab do research using animals?" he asked.

"We certainly do," she told them. "Right now I'm comparing dogs' weight gain as a result of a strictly soy-based diet." She pointed to a row of spotless cages against the far wall. The dogs, all small breeds, looked healthy. They were barking and wagging their tails.

"May I ask where your lab gets its dogs?" asked Frank.

"If you're from an animal rights organization," Beck quickly interjected, "I assure you—"

Joe held up his hand. "Time out," he said. "We're not from any organization." He explained about the dog thefts. "It occurred to us that the thief might be selling the dogs to laboratories— without the labs knowing the dogs were stolen."

"Have you been contacted recently about buying lab animals?" asked Frank.

"Not me," said Dr. Beck.

Jan Skinner leaned back in her chair and frowned. "I was approached," she admitted. "A young man stopped me out in the parking lot, perhaps a week ago. He said he had a source of stray dogs and he was willing to sell them to the lab for two hundred dollars each."

"What did he look like?" asked Joe.

"Young, in his twenties, brown hair."

"Long brown hair?" asked Frank.

"I don't know, it could have been," said Skinner. "He was wearing a hat, one of those woolen sailor's caps. And he never took off his sunglasses."

"Did you buy any of his dogs?"

"Of course not," Dr. Skinner said. "He didn't look to me as though he worked for any reputable supply company. He asked if he could take a card and stay in touch. I told him that would be fine and he left."

"Did you see him go?" Frank asked.

"Actually, I did," Dr. Skinner said. "There was something about him that I didn't trust, so I made sure to escort him out."

"What was he driving?" Joe asked.

Dr. Skinner thought for a moment. "A truck," she said finally. "An old red pickup."

"You gave him a card from the lab," Frank said. "Did he leave a card with you?"

"No. He said they were at the printer's, but he did give me a number." Skinner rooted through the papers on her desk until she found the slip she was looking for. "Here it is." She handed the paper to Frank. "I'm not ever going to use it."

Frank thanked Skinner and Beck and asked them to please call if the young man contacted the lab again. Joe gave Dr. Skinner their phone number.

"You were right," Joe told his brother as he steered the van out onto the main road. "The thief wants to sell the dogs to labs. What a creep!" Joe turned east toward Bayport.

"But who is he?" Frank wanted to know. "Mike Trent could fit the description, but so could Shawn Cabot."

"So could this guy in the rearview mirror," said Joe.

Frank turned around. There was a red pickup truck behind them.

"He looks familiar," said Frank with a wry smile, "like that movie character, the green one with the huge teeth and super powers."

"Since we're not at the movies, let's hope he's wearing a mask," Joe said. "If it's a 'he' at all," he added.

Frank left the passenger seat and crawled into the back of the van for a better look. "He's speeding up," Frank called up to Joe.

The red truck roared up behind the van. The horrible mask never stopped grinning. The driver accelerated and the truck bumped the back of the van.

"Speed up!" Frank urged.

"We're doing seventy now. The road's too narrow," Joe replied. "That guy must be crazy."

Bang! The truck jolted the van again. Frank clambered back up to the passenger's seat and refastened his seat belt.

"That piece of junk's got some power," Joe said. "It looks like he's going to pass us."

"Maybe he wants to run us off the road," warned Frank.

While Joe concentrated on steering, Frank watched as the red truck drew alongside the van. He could see the driver clearly through the truck's open passenger window. If only the guy wasn't wearing that mask. Frank noticed the driver was relaxed enough to steer one-handed. Then he realized the guy's other hand was holding something. In a flash, what it was registered in Frank's brain.

"He's got a gun!" Frank exclaimed.

The masked driver was holding a wicked-looking black semi-automatic. And it was aimed right at Joe.

9 Lowering the Boom

Joe reacted instantly. He slammed the brake pedal to the floor. The van immediately dropped back behind the red truck.

But not fast enough. Not before the masked man fired.

Splat!

The pickup truck disappeared in front of them, lost in a field of red. The windshield was completely covered with red liquid of some kind. Joe couldn't see a thing.

"I can't see the road!" Joe shouted.

He slammed hard on the brake again. He fought the wheel, trying desperately to keep the van on the road. He couldn't remember if the road ahead was straight. The loud thumping told him it wasn't.

"Hang on!" Joe told his brother.

Joe had to do something before he totaled the van. He turned the windshield wipers on high speed and hit the washer switch.

The rubber blades made a full swipe before clearing enough of an area in front of him that he could steer the van back onto firm pavement.

"Great driving," Frank said, patting his brother on the shoulder.

"But the guy in the red pickup got away," Joe complained. "We can't go after him with this red stuff all over the windshield." He pulled over to the shoulder and set the hand brake.

Frank jumped out of the van. He sniffed the heavy red fluid on the windshield. "Latex paint," he said. "The guy had some kind of paint gun."

Frank found some rags in the back of the van. He dipped one in a puddle of standing rain water and attacked the area on the driver's side. Together, they cleaned off as much as they could.

"It'll wash off if we use a pressure hose," said Joe.

"There's a car wash on Center Street," Frank said. While Joe drove, Frank put through the call to the number Dr. Skinner had given them.

"I got an answering machine," Frank said after a minute. "The place is called Bayport Scientific Supply." When he heard the beep, Frank began speaking: "I represent a new lab in Bayport," Frank said. "Our name is Chemical Analysis and Testing, but we're so new, all of our supplies haven't been

78

ordered yet. That's why I'm calling. We're going to need twenty-five dogs for vitamin supplement tests. Can you help us?" Frank left the number of their dad's office machine and hung up.

"Chemical Analysis and Testing?" asked Joe, smiling. "The lab you've just made up that's doing make-believe tests on dogs is called CAT?"

"I thought Dynamic and Organic Guidance would be too obvious," his brother said with a laugh.

Joe turned the van into the car wash. He told the attendant to concentrate on the windows.

"We'll do our best," the man said as he directed Joe to the waiting area.

"Was that Mike Trent who gassed us last night?" Frank asked above the sound of spraying water.

"It was so dark, and it happened so fast, it could've been anyone," Joe said. "I couldn't even see if he had long hair. But it was his apartment, the same address he'd written on his application at Pet Provisions."

"His hair might have been tied back," Frank said. "It could have been under his baseball cap."

"Whoever it was," Joe said, "should know by now we're not going to give up the investigation."

"I think we're dealing with an amateur," Frank said. "He hasn't done anything really serious. The paint gun could have caused an accident, but mostly he's given us headaches. If this was a professional gang, they'd have tried to stop us permanently."

"You're right," Joe agreed. "A professional wouldn't still be looking for a place to sell the dogs. And he would've lined something up *before* stealing the animals."

"I hope we can stop this scam before any of the dogs get hurt," Frank said grimly.

"You know, Trent didn't seem to hold any grudge against George Price for firing him," Joe pointed out. "Don't you think that's a little strange?"

"Trent has a right to be a little resentful," said Frank. "He was hired because of his technical training, then Price hands him a pooper-scooper. You're right, though, Trent didn't gripe."

"Could be an act," Joe commented.

"I've been wondering about Shawn Cabot," Frank mused. "It sounded like he's off from work a lot. That means he had time to steal Spike and to follow us. Why don't we see if he's down at the dry dock today."

Joe drove the now-gleaming van out of the car wash and headed for Bayport's waterfront.

The *Star of Barmet* was covered with workers swarming all over the big cruise ship. Longshoremen pushed loaded dollies up gangways and brought empties back for more.

"Shawn Cabot, right?" the foreman said when Frank and Joe reached his shed. "If you want to talk to Shawn, you're in luck today." He pointed toward the bow of the ship. "He's actually here. He's been off so often, I thought I might have to replace him."

"We'll try not to keep him long," Joe told the foreman.

"I'd appreciate that. He needs to do some work for a change." He handed two hard hats to the Hardys.

Frank thanked him and put on his hat.

Tanned from working outdoors, Shawn Cabot had a gruff, no-nonsense manner about him. His dark hair reached to just below his shirt collar.

Cabot and four other men were securing a load of stateroom furniture to a skid. It was tied with heavy ropes. These in turn were fastened to a steel cable and safety chain. The entire rig would soon be lifted by a boom operating high overhead.

Cabot glanced up at the Hardys as they approached. Joe didn't think Alma Morris's brother looked very happy to have company.

"I don't have the time for this," Cabot said when Frank introduced himself and explained why he and Joe were there. "Besides, I'm not into stealing collies," he added.

"How did you know it was a collie that was stolen?" asked Joe.

"It's really none of your business," Cabot said contemptuously, "but my sister told me. And I'll tell *you* something: if that lousy kennel shuts down because of the theft, I think whoever did it deserves a medal."

"Would you mind telling us what kind of car you drive?" Frank asked.

"Yes, I do mind!" Cabot snapped. "I didn't take the collie, and I'm not answering any of your questions."

"What about your sister?" Joe asked. "There are a lot of people who think she's behind the dognapping."

"Well, she's not!" Cabot shouted. "Anyone who says different answers to me." He waved his fist in Joe's face.

"Calm down," Frank told the young man. "I'm sure you don't want an assault charge against you."

"You stop harassing my sister and there won't be any trouble," Cabot snapped back.

"All we want is the return of the stolen dogs," Joe said.

"Then maybe you ought to talk to those people working nights at the Doghouse Pet Motel," Cabot said, his tone implying the Hardys didn't know anything.

"What people?" Frank wanted to know. "You mean George and Nora Price?"

"I don't know who they are," said Cabot, "and I don't care. But my sister said she was watching last night and there were two people taking dogs out of a truck. She couldn't figure out what they were doing."

"What sort of truck?" asked Joe.

"I didn't ask and she didn't say."

"Was it the company van?" Frank persisted.

"It could have been the presidential limousine," Cabot said sarcastically.

"Shawn?" It was one of the men on Shawn's crew. "We've got to get this load aboard."

"Right," Cabot replied. "I'll be right there." He turned to Frank and Joe. "I've answered enough questions, and so has my sister. I'm telling you, leave her alone."

"I can't promise that," Joe told him. "We'll want to ask her about the dogs she saw last night."

Shawn blew up. "I'm warning you!" he said, practically spitting the words out. "Now get out of here!"

The other men in his crew exchanged looks.

Shawn gave a signal. Nearby, a diesel engine roared to life. Frank automatically stepped back as the slack went out of the cable holding the heavy load of furniture. He grabbed Joe's arm and pulled him away, too.

"We know where he is if we have to find him," Frank said. "Let's go talk to his sister."

Frank started in the direction of the parking area. Joe fell into step beside him. Together they passed through rows of steel racks loaded with large plastic pipes. Suddenly Joe heard a voice from the dock call out, "No! Don't let go of that cable!"

Joe turned around to look. He was trying to spot the source of the trouble when another shout came.

"Look out!" Joe heard.

83

As he turned to Frank, Joe saw a large shadow on the ground. He glanced up.

The skid of stateroom furniture was directly overhead.

"The cable's breaking!" a worker shouted.

Joe could see that the man was right. The safety cable had snapped. The furniture was falling. Joe realized with horror that he and Frank were directly underneath it.

10 Death Threat

Joe made a split-second decision. He grabbed Frank and dragged his brother to the ground. He rolled the two of them under a large steel rack filled with hundreds of six-foot-long plastic pipes.

The skid of furniture crashed to the ground. On the way, one corner of it caught the pipe rack. The top two rows of pipes flew from their places as if there'd been an explosion. The remainder clattered to the ground.

Joe felt the pipes collapsing on top of him and Frank. Just as he'd gambled, the black plastic pipes deflected the skid away from them. The dead weight of falling furniture missed them. When it was over, it took hardly any effort to get out from under the pipes. The sturdy, lightweight plastic pipes simply rolled away.

"Not a scratch," Joe said. "How about you?"

"I told you you'd need those hard hats," the foreman joked nervously as he ran up to Frank and Joe. Several of the workers crowded around. First, one guy started moving the pipes out of the way, then the others joined in.

"That was close," the foreman said. He had a worried look on his face. "That cable must have been faulty."

Frank scanned the dock. Cabot was off working in the background. He was ignoring the accident.

"Shouldn't Shawn be over here checking this out?" Frank asked the foreman. "After all, he was on the crew that got the boom ready."

"I bet he's avoiding us," the foreman suggested. "He probably thinks I'm going blame him."

Joe pushed through the crowd. Cabot started edging away when he saw Joe coming, but Joe was too fast. He sprinted past the hostile young man and blocked his escape.

"I don't suppose you have any idea why that cable snapped," Joe said pointedly to Cabot.

"That's right, I don't," Cabot replied. "Now, leave me alone or something *really* bad will happen to you." He turned and jogged past Joe up the gangplank. Joe watched him disappear onto the first-class deck. Disgusted, Joe rejoined his brother and the foreman.

"Look, we always investigate these things," said the foreman. "If it wasn't an accident, I'll call you."

Joe gave the foreman his name and number and thanked him. With a last look at Shawn Cabot, he and Frank jumped into their van and headed to Alma Morris's place.

"You can stay right out there on the porch," Alma Morris told them when she answered the Hardys' knock. "Shawn told me I shouldn't even talk to you."

"You talked to Shawn?" asked Frank.

"Not even ten minutes ago. Said you two were at the shipyard. He told me that you accused him of trying to kill you." Morris smiled. "My little brother wouldn't hurt a fly."

"Shawn told us you saw a truck and some people with dogs out behind the Doghouse," Frank said, changing the subject. "Was that last night?"

"Sure was," she said. "Something strange about it, too."

"Exactly what did you see?" asked Joe.

"A really ugly couple. I hate to say that about anyone, and the light *was* bad, but these two looked like something out of a horror movie. I thought they might be wearing rubber masks." She gave a short laugh. "I *hope* they were wearing masks."

"How many dogs did they have?" Frank pressed.

"Seven, eight, maybe," she said. "It was hard to tell. They took the dogs out of the truck and walked them around. I went to the kitchen to heat up some milk, so I didn't see what happened to them. Next time I looked, the people and the dogs were gone.

"What time did you see this?"

"It was maybe three-thirty, three forty-five in the morning. I couldn't sleep," she explained.

"You said they took the dogs out of a truck," Frank said. "Was this the company van?"

"No, it was a *truck* truck. A pickup," Morris said, "a really beat-up one."

"Did you see what color it was?" Joe asked Morris.

"It was pretty dark out, but the truck looked red to me."

Frank and Joe exchanged a glance.

"Did you wake up Shawn and tell him what was going on?" Joe pressed.

"There you go again!" Joe could see that Morris was getting annoyed. "Trying to pin this thing on me and my brother." She started to slam the door, but Joe blocked it with his foot.

"He was home, wasn't he?" Joe asked firmly.

"He was asleep in bed!" Morris screamed. She stomped on Joe's foot. When he flinched, she pushed him out of the way and slammed the door.

"If Morris is telling the truth, it wasn't Shawn who locked us in the pet carriers and gassed us," Joe said. He walked slowly down the porch steps and out to the street.

"But Morris's information does connect the red

88

truck to the Doghouse," Frank added. "Now we've got to find out who's driving it."

"As long as we're in the neighborhood," said Frank, "let's walk over to the Doghouse."

Dana Bailey was on the phone when Frank and Joe entered the office. She said, "Thank you," and hung up.

"How's the investigation coming?" she asked.

"It won't be long now," said Frank.

"Really?" Dana asked. "That's great."

"There are still a few loose ends," Joe said.

"You've been working the night shift, right?" Frank asked.

"Yes, but I'm pulling a double shift today. Nora's meeting with the advertising people at the *Banner.* George wants to run a promotion, something to drum up business."

Joe cleared his throat. "We were told someone brought several dogs in here yesterday morning."

"Nora was on duty yesterday," Dana said. "She came on at six-thirty."

"This was earlier," Frank said. "Around three-thirty."

"I didn't hear anything," Dana said. "Who'd you get this from?"

"We can't tell you that," Joe said.

"You got it from Alma Morris!" Dana exclaimed.

"Like Joe said, we can't tell you," Frank said.

Dana was angry. "She probably made the whole thing up."

"Why would she do that?"

"To throw suspicion onto someone else, that's why," Dana said, pushing the words through her clenched jaw. Then, like a cloud rolling across the sun, a change came over Dana's face. She looked guilty all of a sudden.

"Is something wrong?" asked Joe.

"Promise me you won't say anything," she said.

Frank glanced at Joe. "About what?"

"It's hard working nights," Dana said. "Sometimes I doze off, you know what I mean? I could lose my job if you say anything."

"Are you saying you were asleep last night?" Frank asked Dana.

"I might have been," she admitted. "I've done it before. And since Price fired Iola, I've been putting in extra time."

"If you don't mind," Joe said, "we'll look around the kennel again."

"No problem," she said. Dana jumped down from her stool behind the counter and unlocked the kennel door.

Frank wandered to the far end of the room. The cages lining both sides of the aisle were filled. "Business looks good," he commented.

"It's picked up," Dana said. "But Mr. Price still wants to buy a newspaper ad."

Frank opened a can of dog treats and fed them to the dogs. They wagged their tails and barked. A couple even sat up and begged for seconds.

While leaning down to hand a dog biscuit to a golden retriever, Frank noticed the owner's name was typed onto a tiny piece of paper and slipped into a metal receptacle. But there wasn't any name on the cage next to it.

"Who is this dog's owner?" he asked Dana.

"I haven't gotten them all typed up yet," she said, then reddened. "You've sort of caught me lying down on the job today," she added. "Please don't say anything to Mr. Price. I really need this job. I've got my car, the rent on my apartment . . ." She trailed off and looked beseechingly at Frank.

"I hate to tell you," Joe said, "but there are several dogs that still need logging in." He was looking at the papers on a clipboard hanging near the office door. "There are twelve dogs listed, and there must be twenty or so in here."

"I know," she said softly. "I'll get on it."

Dana practically leapt through the door when the phone rang in the office. "Excuse me," she said.

Joe was still looking through the kennel's paperwork when Dana poked her head back inside the kennel.

"It's for you," she said, surprise in her voice.

Frank stepped into the office and took the receiver from Dana.

"Frank Hardy here," he said. That was the last thing Joe heard him say. The remainder of the conversation was all one-sided. Finally, Frank handed the phone back to Dana. He didn't say goodbye.

"Is something wrong?" she asked him.

"What is it?" Joe wanted to know. He closed the kennel door and stepped into the office.

"Whoever it was wasn't very pleased with us," Frank said. "I was told to stop investigating the missing dogs or something terrible would happen."

"Did you recognize the voice?" Joe asked.

"No," Frank admitted. "It was muffled. But there's more," he added. "The caller said if we don't stop the investigation right now, the next time we see Spike, he'll be a dead dog."

11 Roll Over and Play Dead

"The thief was very clear," Frank said. "If we don't give up right now, Spike is dead."

"Maybe you'd better do what he says," Dana suggested.

Joe looked at Dana. "What makes you think it's a 'he'?" he asked.

The question startled Dana. "I just assumed it was a guy," she said. "I didn't mean anything by it. Women can be thieves, too."

"If it makes you feel any better," Frank said, letting Dana off the hook, "we've assumed it was a man from the start. But the voice on the phone was muffled, so it's difficult to be sure."

"What about that Shawn Cabot guy?" Dana

93

asked. "He could be doing Morris's dirty work for her."

"We've thought about that," Joe said. "How about Mike Trent? Have you heard from him recently?"

"Why would I hear from him?" Dana asked. "We worked together, Price fired him, that's it."

"Did Trent drive to work?" asked Frank.

"I think so," Dana said. "But I never really paid any attention."

"You didn't see his truck?" Frank asked slyly.

"Truck, car," she said, "I have no idea what he was driving."

"What about Shawn Cabot?" Joe asked. "You told us you'd seen him leave the house a couple of times."

"Yes," she said. "He was waiting for the bus. There's a stop right out front." Dana picked up a pile of papers. "Listen, guys, I've really got to get this paperwork done before Nora comes on duty. It's just Nora and me now since Mr. Price went to New York on business. I think he's working on his big franchising deal."

"We won't hold you up any more," Frank told her. "But tell Nora to keep her ears open, and," he added, "you might want to stay awake."

Dana nodded as she walked with Frank and Joe to the door.

"How did the dognapper know we were there?"

Frank asked when they were back in the van. He looked around, wondering if the person was nearby.

"How long was Dana on the phone before she called to say it was for us?" asked Joe.

"Just seconds," Frank replied. He checked the rearview mirror, then drove out into traffic. "Why, do you think Dana has something to do with this? You think she told the caller we were there?"

"It's possible," Joe said. "I wasn't really paying attention, but I think all she did was pick up the phone and say 'hello.'"

The Hardys' discussion about Dana's phone conversation was interrupted by the buzzing of their own car phone.

"Iola's back!" Joe whispered after answering the call. He held his hand over the mouthpiece. "She's at our house right now, and she wants to pick up Spike. What should I tell her?"

"Tell her we'll be right home." Frank headed immediately for the expressway, the shortest route home.

Joe braced himself for the worst when he entered the living room and saw Iola.

"Where's Spike?" Iola asked. "Usually he comes running right up to me."

"We can explain," Joe said nervously. "Just sit down and listen."

Joe saw a look of alarm cross Iola's face as she sat down on the couch. While Joe told Iola the whole story, Frank went out to the kitchen and got three sodas.

Iola got right to the point. "So who's got Spike—Mike Trent or Shawn Cabot?"

"We need evidence before we accuse anyone," Frank reminded her.

"I know." Iola let out a long sigh. "It's just that if something happens to Spike, I'll feel terrible."

"I've been thinking," Joe said. "If either the red truck or the gray sedan belongs to Shawn Cabot, wouldn't we have seen at least one of them parked at the dry dock?"

"Good point," Frank said. "But he might have parked somewhere away from the dry dock."

The entire group jumped when a phone rang once in another part of the Hardy home.

"It's Dad's fax machine," Frank said. He got up and went down the hall to their father's office. The machine was finished printing the fax when Frank reached the tray.

"Anything for us?" Joe called out.

"Sure is," said Frank. "It's from the courthouse. Guess who owns the warehouse?"

"I give up," Joe said when he joined his brother in the office.

"Royal Restorations Corporation."

Joe shrugged. "And . . ."

"Royal Restorations is owned by the same company that runs the dry dock."

Frank handed the fax to Joe.

Joe read over the sheet. "It also says that practically every warehouse and storefront on Limehouse and Water Streets are owned by RRC."

"That means Shawn Cabot could easily have known about the warehouse," Frank said. "Dock workers may even have permission to use it."

Back in the kitchen the regular phone rang. "Do you want me to answer that?" Iola called.

"Please," Joe said. He and Frank started back toward the kitchen when he heard Iola's voice.

"This is Iola Morton," Joe heard Iola tell the caller, then she screamed into the receiver. "You'll go to prison for life!"

"Who is that?" asked Joe.

Iola slammed down the phone.

"This guy, this creep, said we've got fifteen minutes to make up our minds," she said, fury in her voice. "We can have Spike back only if we pay him five hundred dollars and stop investigating."

"He'll return Spike?" asked Frank.

"It sounded that way," Iola confirmed. "He told me he'll call back."

It was a tense quarter hour in the Hardy house. The minute the phone rang, Joe grabbed it.

"What's your decision?" the muffled voice demanded. Joe thought the caller was probably talking through a towel.

"We want Spike back," Joe told the thief. "We'll do whatever you say."

While Joe and the dognapper were talking, Frank

slipped over to the caller ID box in Fenton Hardy's office. He wrote down the number of the phone the dognapper had called from. Then, using one of his dad's business lines, Frank called the phone company. The operator told Frank that the number was assigned to a pay phone on Bay Street. Bay Street was in the waterfront district.

"We not only want Spike, but all of the other dogs you've stolen," Frank heard Joe telling the thief when he returned to the living room.

"I'm only going to say this one more time," the dognapper growled. "I give you Spike, and you give me five hundred dollars. And then you back off."

"What about the other dogs?" Joe asked.

"If I give you back Spike and you don't keep your word, then I will kill one of the dogs every day. The collie will be the first to die." He paused. "Any more questions?" the thief asked.

"No," Joe told the dognapper.

"Smart fellow," the person said. "Now, here's what I want you to do."

"Keep your shirt on," Joe said. "I need some paper." He picked up a note pad from the counter.

"Okay, let's hear it," he told the dognapper.

As the dognapper gave instructions, Joe repeated them aloud. "Lookout Point, midnight tonight," Joe said as he wrote.

"Park in the east parking lot," the voice said. "Roll down the front windows on both the driver's and passenger's sides. And wait. You'll be given further instructions."

Frank paced and Iola sat tensely on the couch while Joe scribbled on the pad.

"And if you don't follow my instructions to the last little detail," the voice growled, "I'll give the dog an injection that puts him to sleep. Forever. If that happens, the next call you get from me will be to tell you where you can pick up Spike's corpse."

"You're a real tough guy," Joe said with contempt, "threatening a dog."

"Yeah, yeah," said the thief. "Save it for someone who cares. You do what you're told, and no one gets hurt. Did you get it all?"

"I've got it," Joe said.

"That's good," the dognapper said. "But I forgot one thing."

"What's that?" Joe asked.

"You and your brother stay out of this," he said. "I'll make the switch only if you're not there."

"Then how will you make the switch?" Joe asked warily.

"Tell that Morton girl to be at the park tonight at midnight," the thief said. "And tell her she'd better come alone."

12 Every Dog Has
Its Night

Joe glanced over at Iola. She was nervously twirling a strand of her dark hair. Before Joe could respond, the dognapper had hung up.

Joe slowly replaced the receiver. He hated putting Iola in danger, but it was the only way. After explaining the dognapper's demands to Frank and Iola, he put his arm around his anxious girlfriend and gave her a quick hug.

"Spike is coming home alive," Joe told Iola firmly. "I give you my word."

"Joe's right," Frank said. "If our thief expects five hundred dollars when he returns Spike, it means he'll be there when it happens. We'll be there, too, and we'll nail the sucker."

"He said I have to come alone," Iola pointed out.

"You will be alone," Frank said, "but the thief won't. He will be in the middle of the trap we're going to set for him."

"Don't forget the ransom money," Joe reminded his brother. "I'll drive down to the bank."

"While you're out," Frank said, "Iola and I will fix supper. I'll put hamburgers on the grill, and we can have some baked beans."

"I can make the salad," Iola said.

"I think there's still some of Aunt Gertrude's lemon pie in the fridge," Joe said. "Save me a piece."

Joe hurried out to the van and drove to the branch of his bank that stayed open late. It was five minutes to closing when he parked and made his way to a teller. He filled out the withdrawal slip while he stood in line. When he reached the window, he asked the young woman to give him the five hundred in twenty-dollar bills.

"Hey, Joe Hardy!" a voice behind him said.

Joe turned around. He found himself face-to-face with Mike Trent. Trent was holding a withdrawal slip and a pay stub.

"Looks like you're getting ready for a big night on the town," Trent joked. He was looking at Joe's thick wad of bills.

"I wanted enough to cover the movie and a bag of popcorn," Joe quipped.

"And maybe a large soda, too," Trent added. His face became serious. "You guys had a break on that missing dog case yet?"

"Not a thing," Joe told him.

Trent nodded. "Too bad. But sometimes you've got to know when to quit."

"I guess," said Joe. "How's Maude Macklin? Anything unusual over at Pet Provisions?"

"Somebody broke in last night," Trent said. "A couple of large pet carriers were damaged."

"I heard you've moved," Joe said, changing the subject. He didn't want to be reminded of his tiny prison. "You used to live down on the waterfront, didn't you?"

"Sure did," Trent said. "Too many break-ins in the neighborhood."

Joe started to ask him where he was living, but Mike interrupted and said he had to run. The two shook hands and Trent hurried out of the bank.

Late that night Joe and Iola went over the plan one more time. An hour earlier Frank had taken the van and hurried down to the marina where the brothers kept their powerboat, the *Sleuth*. At eleven-thirty, Iola left for the park. Joe waited ten minutes, then got into his father's sedan and drove off.

In case someone had the house under surveillance, Joe headed south, away from Lookout Point. When he was sure he wasn't being followed, Joe turned back toward Shore Road, the most direct route to Lookout Point.

The night sky over Barmet Bay was moonless. Joe cruised along slowly until he spotted a rest stop that was heavily shaded. He glided to a stop. After locking the car, he hiked over to the east lot. Iola's car was parked in the shadows under a pair of ancient beech trees. He could see Iola sitting in the driver's seat. The rest of the park was empty.

Joe slipped into a grove of trees. He knelt down and watched.

At first he thought the movement was an illusion, something caused by the fog and the lights that were meant to illuminate the asphalt.

Then Joe saw it again. It was a person. He was dressed in black and moving through the trees toward Iola's car. Joe squinted, trying to get a better look.

Suddenly the man broke out of the shadows and made straight for Iola. Joe tensed, ready to leap out if she was threatened. The man tossed something through the passenger's window of Iola's car. What was it? And who was this guy? Should he rush him? Joe wondered.

Stick to the plan, he told himself.

Joe sighed with relief when the runner passed Iola's car without stopping.

"Joe?" It was Iola. Joe adjusted the tiny earphone. Iola was wearing a hidden microphone and a miniature transmitter in the pouch of her fanny pack.

"I hear you," he whispered. "Is everything okay?"

"So far, so good," she said. "That guy threw a note in my window." Joe heard the rustle of paper, then Iola read the note out loud. When she finished, Joe asked her if she'd gotten a good look at the jogger.

"No. He was running away from me. All I saw was his back."

"Go ahead and follow the instructions," Joe said, "and I won't be far away."

"If I get my hands on him, it's the dognapper that's going to need your protection," she said.

"Don't forget," Joe reminded her. "Be cool."

The instructions said to wait five minutes before getting out of the car. To Joe, it felt more like five hours before he saw the light go on in Iola's car. She opened the door and got out. Without glancing in Joe's direction, Iola walked purposefully out of the parking lot. She patted her fanny pack, indicating to Joe that she had the ransom with her. The dognapper's message told her to meet him out at the point.

Joe watched uneasily as Iola headed toward the stairs that led up to the observation deck. When the switch took place, Iola would be on a wooden platform, high out over the bay. Joe couldn't be sure, but he guessed Iola would be a good four hundred feet above the rocky shore below.

Joe waited for a count of twenty, letting Iola get to the stairs and start climbing. Then, keeping as hidden as he could, Joe began making his way after her. Even though the dognapper had told Iola she was going to be watched the entire time, Joe believed the operation was strictly amateur. There might be two thieves, but he'd seen no evidence to confirm a whole gang. That meant the bad guys would be spread pretty thin.

The note said that Iola was to walk out onto the observation deck. Joe peered ahead and saw Iola's shadowy form ahead in the fog. Joe had to strain to see her as she seemed to move in and out of the mist.

"You miserable thief!" a voice shouted. Joe recognized it as Iola's. "You promised you'd give me Spike!"

Joe froze. What was wrong? The plan called for Iola to wait quietly until the thief approached. "Iola," he spoke into his tiny microphone, "what's happening?"

Suddenly Iola shrieked. Her piercing voice cut through the moist, heavy air. Joe knew the sound of terror when he heard it. He heard her start to call out again, then there was a thumping sound. Joe's earphone went dead.

Silence descended over the park.

Joe ran in the direction of the sound. He reached the beginning of the wooden walkway that led out onto the deck. Joe had spent many weekends at the park. He knew the area well. But he'd spent most of his time here during the day. Now Joe found himself staring into a dense fog. He could see the end of his nose, but he didn't see anything beyond.

Joe knew he had to reach Iola, even if it meant revealing his presence and blowing the original plan. The strange sounds he was hearing told him the plan was already in shambles.

"Iola," he called, "hang on!"

Joe sprang up onto the deck. It was completely shrouded in fog. Frantically, Joe searched the area. Where was she? There was no sign of Iola, and no sign of the dognapper either.

"Iola?" he called. Joe leaned out over the edge of the deck. He stepped out onto the landing at the top of the many flights of stairs down to the beach.

Nothing.

Joe called her name again and again. "Iola, can you hear me?"

The silence was eerie.

Panic seized Joe. What had happened to her? Only seconds before he'd heard two people on the deck. Where were they? And what had happened to Spike?

Out on Barmet Bay, Frank throttled back the *Sleuth*'s engine. He knew sound traveled fast over water, and he didn't want the dognapper alerted to the two-pronged trap. Joe's assignment was to cut off the thief's escape by land. Frank planned to seal off the long flights of stairs that led from the platform down to the beach.

Frank eased the boat alongside the narrow pier. He looped a line around one of the supports, then tied the rope tightly. The *Sleuth* rocked gently against the tires that had been placed there to protect boat hulls from damage.

An older man and a young couple walking hand in hand were the only people remaining on the beach. Frank surveyed the sand in both directions to make sure, then turned his attention to the narrow stairway leading to the observation deck. The deck itself, he saw, was already obscured by the darkness and the fog rolling in. By the time he reached the first flight of steps, the beach, the dock, the *Sleuth*, and the people were fading into the mist.

Frank froze. Somewhere up above he heard a noise. Was it Iola? Joe?

Frank started up the stairs. He took the first flight two steps at a time. When he reached the landing and leapt onto the second step, the wood gave way. Frank's right knee slammed hard against the next step, and he gasped at the sudden pain. He slumped on the step, willing the pain away.

There was a throbbing ache in Frank's knee every

time he tried to put pressure on his foot, but he had no time to waste.

He was working his way up the steep wooden stairs when he heard the scream again. He leaned back over the railing and craned his neck, scanning upward. All he could see was the next set of steps disappearing into the fog. Gritting his teeth, he increased his speed.

Gasping for breath, Frank reached the deck and searched frantically for any sign of his brother or Iola.

"Iola!" he called. "Joe?"

"Frank? Over here." It was Joe. Frank was relieved to see him step out the fog.

"Where's Iola?" Frank asked. "I thought I heard a struggle."

"I don't know," Joe admitted. "She was with the dognapper, but something went wrong."

"So much for the big plan," Frank said. He kicked at a post, then winced as pain shot through his knee. "We didn't get Spike back, and now we've lost Iola."

"The thief can't have taken Iola very far," Joe told his brother. "Let's split up. You take the area north of the deck, I'll search south."

Joe knew he sounded more confident than he felt. He'd scoured the cliff's edge twice already and hadn't found a clue. Iola hadn't dropped anything, and neither had her attacker. *If* she had been attacked, Joe thought. Iola might have gotten away.

Suddenly Joe stopped. He knew where Iola might be. He'd just remembered.

The caves! Barmet Cliff was riddled with caves. Iola might be hiding in one of them.

Joe ran along the edge of the cliff, looking for a path or any access to the granite face. He had to be careful. One slip and he'd be gone.

On the left Joe saw a break in the shrubs. Was it a path? Joe was heading for the opening when he heard a sound behind him. Relief flooded through him. It had to be Iola.

Before Joe could turn, a swinging chain snaked around his neck. Someone behind him yanked hard, pulling Joe off his feet. As the chain tightened, Joe coughed.

He reached up to loosen the chain but as he did, the assailant forced a rag roughly over Joe's face. The rag had a powerful medicinal smell. Joe fought blindly, but it was too late. A heavy dizziness fell over him. Everything was spinning. Can't fall over the cliff, was the last thought he had before he sank into oblivion.

13 Noises in the Dark

Frank was having no luck. When he saw two figures appear out of the fog, he felt sure it must be Joe and Iola. Relieved, he ran in their direction, only to pull up short. It wasn't them at all.

It was the couple he'd seen down on the beach. They shrank away from Frank, obviously thinking he meant them harm.

Frank held out his hands. "I'm sorry," he said. "I didn't mean to startle you, but have you seen anyone else around here? I'm looking for my brother and his girlfriend."

The man seemed wary. "No," he answered shortly. The guy put his arm around his date and they hurried away.

"Joe!" Frank called into the fog. There was no

reply, and when Frank looked around, he was alone. Where had Joe gone?

Frank felt like kicking himself. He'd left his multicell flashlight down in the *Sleuth's* locker. Moving as fast as his sore knee allowed, Frank hurried back down the stairs. He clambered onto the boat, grabbed the flashlight, and started back up.

He was winded from his second trip up the rickety stairs. When he finally made it back up to the observation deck, his knee was throbbing badly.

The flashlight usually threw a penetrating beam, but just as the heavy fog cut down on visibility, the damp air seemed to absorb the light. Frank checked both sides and every inch of the wooden walkway and scoured the deck itself, but he couldn't find a thing. He let out a long, frustrated sigh.

"Here we go again," he muttered. He made it down the stairs leading to the parking lot and Iola's car.

Frank sagged against the side of the sedan. Things were looking pretty bleak. First Iola had disappeared, and now his brother was missing. And there'd been no sign of Spike.

Frank knew this was no time to give up. He located the spot where Joe had parked their father's car. Using the cellular phone, he called the police. Fortunately, Con Riley was on duty. Riley told Frank he'd be at the park in minutes.

Riley was as good as his word. The air was so

heavy that Frank didn't hear the police siren until the car was practically in the parking lot.

Frank gave Detective Riley and the officer who had responded to the call with him the important details.

"How long have Iola and Joe been missing?" Riley asked.

Frank looked at his watch. "Twenty minutes," he said.

"Let's fan out," Con said. "Officer Johnson, you take the cliff on both sides of the walkway. Frank and I will check the parking lots."

Frank had already searched the east lot where they were, so he told Riley he'd take the west parking area.

The west lot was shrouded by trees and tall bushes. The fog diffused the mercury vapor light, making the area look like a black-and-white movie.

Since Iola was told to park in the east lot, Frank thought it possible the dognapper planned to use the west lot. He checked the pavement for clues. Nothing.

Although Frank was tired and discouraged, he knew he couldn't stop looking. He knew Iola's and Joe's lives might depend upon it. He rubbed his aching knee for a moment, then continued searching for clues.

Joe's head ached ferociously. He tried to feel around for a knot or bump.

He couldn't. He was tied up.

Then he remembered the rag. He hadn't been hit. He'd been drugged or gassed. That's what was causing his headache.

He heard a scratching sound. Joe forced his eyes open, but he couldn't see a thing. He was blind-folded.

Anger welled up in Joe. He was angry at the thief who kept knocking him out. He was more angry at himself for being the victim.

And where was Iola? Was she making those sounds?

He started to call out to her, then decided against it. He didn't know where he was, or who might be here with him. The bad guy could still be around. He decided to keep quiet and work on the ropes.

A weary Frank suggested that he and Officers Johnson and Riley scour the area one more time.

"I want to find them as much as you," Riley assured Frank, "but we've been over this park with a fine-tooth comb."

"One more time, please, Con?" Frank begged.

Officer Riley held Frank's gaze. Then he nodded, and the three fellows split up again.

Frank headed for the observation deck. After all, he thought, that was the place where Iola, the dognapper, and Joe were last seen.

Most of the ground at the cliff's edge fell away sharply. Frank searched until he found a break in the jagged outcroppings. He eased himself down beneath the observation platform. It reminded him of the crawl space under a front porch.

Frank could tell from the marks and debris in the dirt that he was not the first person to make the treacherous descent. Frank moved the flashlight beam across the ground.

Something silver sparkled in the distance.

Frank crawled forward along the uneven ground. He brushed against the thick joists overhead.

Stretching out toward the object, Frank snagged it with two fingers. He dragged it back and held it under the light. It was Joe's watch.

Frank looked back to the spot where he'd seen the watch. It was only inches from the edge of the cliff. Had it fallen from the deck above? Or had the dognapper grabbed Joe in the dark and pushed him over the cliff?

Joe was having some luck with the ropes. Whoever had tied them had done a good job, but Joe knew his persistence was paying off.

He heard the scratching sound again, but there were no other noises. Finally, he pulled his right hand free. He'd heard no evidence of his kidnapper, so Joe untied the ropes around his wrists, then pulled the blindfold loose.

He was in a dark room. The only illumination came from tiny beams of light coming in through cracks in the darkened windows. The glass appeared to have been painted over. Joe wondered if he was in Alma Morris's garage.

When his eyes adjusted to the dim light, Joe made out a lawnmower, a workbench with rusty tools, and containers of lawn chemicals. He spotted a dented can of charcoal-lighting fluid, and a gallon bottle with a couple of inches of amber liquid in the bottom.

Ordinary enough, Joe thought. But when he turned his head to look across to the other side of the garage, he saw a gray car. Joe got up slowly, head still pounding, and walked around it. Just as he expected, the car had one yellow door.

In the far corner of the garage, something moved. Joe froze and peered over the hood of the car. He noticed a large, lumpy tarpaulin. When it moved again, Joe heard a moan. He stepped quickly to the canvas. Snatching a corner, he threw the tarp aside.

Joe stared down at Iola. She was bound and gagged, lying on a pile of lawn furniture cushions.

Joe removed the gag and untied the rope around her hands.

"Are you all right?" Joe asked Iola.

"Now that you've found me," she told him. She stood up shakily. "Where are we?"

"We're in someone's garage. And I'm beginning to figure out why Dana didn't want us to see her car or where she lived." He started to say more, but he

115

heard the scratching sound again. This time it was accompanied by a bark. He and Iola looked at each other and smiled.

"That was a dog!" Iola exclaimed. She looked around the garage.

"It's coming from behind those trash bags," Joe said, pointing past the car.

They picked their way through the debris to the other side of the garage. Iola reached the pet carriers first. There were at least two dozen dogs of all sizes. Joe found more behind what looked like two years' worth of newspapers stacked nearly to the ceiling. In each pet carrier was a dog. Joe thought it was strange that most of them seemed to be sleeping. They've been drugged, he realized.

"These are the stolen dogs," Iola said. "They have to be." She knelt down beside a cage in which a small terrier was scratching frantically. When her face got close to the steel mesh, the terrier began wagging its tail and let out a sharp bark. A few of the other dogs began stirring, and the garage began to fill with the sounds of dogs barking, yelping, and moving around in their cages.

"Whatever they are," Joe said, "all this noise is going to alert our captor—if he's still around. We've got to get them to be quiet."

"I can't stand seeing them locked up," Iola said angrily. She began to speak soothingly through the bars, trying to quiet the terrier.

One bark was louder, more insistent than the

116

others. It was coming from a cage in a corner. Joe pushed aside a bag of lawn clippings to clear a path. Iola was right behind him.

Joe leaned down. The dog looked familiar. Iola reached out and opened the carrier.

The dog sprang through the opening. It raced past Joe to Iola. The dog jumped up, placing its paws on Iola's legs. Clearly, the dog knew Iola. And just as clearly, Iola recognized the dog.

"We've found him," Iola said excitedly. "We've found Spike!"

14 Out of Her Misery

Back at the park, Frank was exhausted. He was sitting in his father's car, talking over the kidnapping with Officer Riley. They'd searched the park thoroughly. Then they'd searched it again.

"I never thought people could just disappear," Riley said, "until now."

Frank didn't say anything. He kept turning his brother's watch over and over. Then it hit him. "The caves," he said. He looked up at Detective Riley. "I don't know why I didn't think of it before. The cliffs are full of caves."

"There are hundreds of caves," Riley said. "You think the dognapper is hiding Joe and Iola in one of those?"

"Where else could they have gone?" Frank

asked. "I'd have heard him take them down the steps. And I found Joe's watch *under* the deck. We've been looking in all the wrong places."

"It's too dark and foggy to reach the caves now," Riley pointed out, "let alone search them. It's dangerous enough in the daylight. But if you think that's where they are, I'll have the Coast Guard watch from the water side, and we can station a couple of black-and-whites up here."

"The *Sleuth*'s still tied up at the dock," Frank said.

"I'll have it taken back to the marina," Riley told him. "Now go home and get some rest. If it turns out to be a kidnapping, the kidnappers might call your house anyway."

"You're probably right," Frank told Riley. He gave the officer his boat keys. "I hate to give up, though."

"At least call home and let someone know where you are," Riley said. "You've been out all night and your folks are probably worried sick."

Frank nodded absently. Luckily, his parents were still out of town, and Aunt Gertrude was a heavy sleeper. But he knew the policeman wouldn't be persuaded to search the caves now, so Frank started his father's sedan and pulled onto Shore Road.

Call home . . . call home. Where had he heard that before, Frank thought. Riley had just said it, of course, but somehow it rang a bell.

Frank picked up the cellular phone. Instead of

making the call, though, he pulled over onto the shoulder and sat, thinking. He replayed the case in his head. He went over the details of where they'd been, what they'd heard.

Call home . . .

Then he remembered. The first morning he and Joe were at the Doghouse, the morning they learned about the theft of the collie, Dana Bailey had excused herself to call home. It all came back now. Frank remembered her saying she needed to tell her parents where she was and that she was going to have to work an extra shift. But later she mentioned being worried about paying the rent on her apartment. And when he and Joe had met her in downtown Bayport, she hadn't wanted them to come to her place because her apartment was messy. Frank realized that if he and Joe had picked her up at her place, they might remember she'd lied about needing to phone her parents.

No doubt about it—Dana Bailey had lied.

Whoever she had called, it sure wasn't her parents.

It was the dognapper!

Dana Bailey, Frank remembered, had been surprised to find out that Frank and Joe were friends of Iola. That was why she had had to use the phone. She had wanted to tell her accomplice that the Hardys were on the case. How else could the thief have gotten on their trail so fast? Frank figured Dana had also told the dognapper about Iola taking care of Spike. Then the thief had probably followed Frank and Joe to their house. While they'd been inside getting lunch, the dognapper had taken Spike out of the yard.

But why? Suddenly, it made sense to Frank. When Dana realized the Hardys were looking for the collie, she knew she was in trouble. Frank remembered how impressed Dana was with the Hardys. They had a reputation for catching criminals. It might take a while before stolen mutts got the attention of the police, but Frank and Joe were helping a friend, so they'd be really motivated. Dana must have wondered how she could drive them from the case. If Spike was dognapped, Dana and her accomplice could use him to convince Frank and Joe to back off. Spike would be a bargaining tool. But something must have gone wrong, and now it had gone far beyond dognapping. Kidnapping, if that's what had happened to Iola and Joe, was a federal offense.

Frank wondered what had happened at the park. Why the change of plan? Had Iola or Joe identified the dognapper? Did the thief now think he had to get rid of the witnesses?

Frank pulled out onto the road and pressed down on the accelerator. He headed straight for the Doghouse. He knew there was still a lot he hadn't put together, but one thing was sure: Dana Bailey was the key to Joe and Iola's disappearance.

* * *

Iola's happy reunion with Spike was short-lived. Someone was at the door of the garage. The moment Joe heard a key in the lock, he looked for a place he and Iola could hide. He figured anyone with a key wasn't there to help. He caught Iola's eye and she nodded, letting him know she had also heard the person at the door.

As Iola ducked out of sight behind a large patio table, Joe slipped behind the door.

Spike looked from Iola to Joe, then stood by the dog carriers and growled.

A man entered the garage. Light from the outside shone into the widening space of the open door. "What the—" Joe heard the man say. Light flashed over the spot where Joe had been only seconds before.

Behind the door, Joe held his breath as the man took a few steps farther into the garage. Joe could see the light from his flashlight darting around the room.

The man took several more steps inside, and Joe made his move. He sprang from behind the door, slamming it shut. He grabbed the man's left arm and wrenched it back.

The man was surprised, but he was also fast. He swung his flashlight up and back over his shoulder. One end of the light delivered a blow to the side of Joe's head.

Joe was stunned, and as he wobbled, he let go of the guy's arm. The man turned to face him, and Joe saw that once again his assailant was wearing a rubber mask. He looked as eerie and grotesque as an alien in a science fiction movie.

The man was coming toward Joe, wielding the flashlight. Over the guy's shoulder, Joe saw Iola in her hiding place near the back of the garage. She scrambled out from under the table.

The assailant must have heard her, because his head whipped around toward the sound. Joe leapt for him, but in a swift move the man brought the flashlight sharply across Joe's face.

Joe saw stars. His knees buckled and he went down. He could hear Spike barking, but Joe couldn't tell where Iola was.

The dognapper could, though. He turned from Joe and raced toward Iola. Joe was struggling to his feet when the masked man made a flying tackle and dragged Iola down in a heap. As he did, he must have dropped the flashlight because Joe heard a smash and everything went dark.

"Iola," Joe shouted. He tried to move in the direction of Iola and the attacker, but he was still woozy and couldn't move very fast. Joe could just make out their shapes. It looked as if the attacker was pinning Iola down and winding a rope around her wrists.

"Help!" Iola screamed.

Joe saw the attacker stuff a wad of cloth in Iola's mouth and drag her over behind the pet carriers.

Joe wondered if he should make a break for it

while he had the chance to go and get some help, but he decided he just couldn't leave Iola alone with this creep. With renewed energy, Joe rushed across the garage. The masked man neatly side-stepped Joe, then kicked him. Joe fell to the floor, landing in a pile of junk that came crashing down on top of him.

"Iola?" Joe called, knocking off some of the debris. He tried to sit up and instantly felt the man yank his wrists. Before Joe could react, the man was wrapping sticky electrical tape around Joe's wrists.

"Thought you were pretty smart, didn't you?" the masked man said.

"Are you crazy?" Joe asked his captor. "Stealing dogs is one thing, but what makes you think you can get away with kidnapping people?"

"It's all your girlfriend's fault," the man told Joe. "If she'd just given me the money, I'd have told her where to pick up Spike. She had to be the hero, though, and capture the big bad dog thief all by herself."

"You'll be in custody soon enough," Joe assured him.

"Yeah, right," the thief said sarcastically. "Even if that were true, there won't be anyone left to testify. As soon as I take care of a couple of details, I'll be out of here."

"You're going to leave your accomplice behind?" Joe asked on a hunch.

"She doesn't—" The masked man stopped.

"Very good, Hardy," he said smoothly. "You almost tricked me. Well, no matter. You see, your meddling in my business means that one of the details I have to attend to is you. You and Iola."

"What are you talking about?" Joe demanded.

"I'm sorry to have to tell you this," the dognapper said, "but you've given me no choice. I really have to dispose of you both."

15 Put to Sleep

"Iola?" Joe called out across the dark garage. All he heard in response was a muffled voice. Then he remembered that the dognapper had gagged her. Joe tried to twist the electrical tape, but it was wound tightly.

"Now, the good news is, the dogs will still be alive this time tomorrow." The dognapper paused dramatically, then went on. "The bad news is, you and the girl won't."

Joe thought if he could stall and keep the guy talking, he and Iola might have a chance. Maybe he'd be able to buy them enough time to come up with some kind of plan.

"It won't be long until my brother gets here," Joe said, bluffing.

"Your brother doesn't have a clue about where you are," the dognapper said.

The guy had a point. Joe concentrated on the man's voice. Was it Shawn Cabot? It didn't really sound like Shawn's voice, but Joe wasn't sure yet. And this could be Alma Morris's garage.

"How'd you get into the dog-stealing business?" Joe asked, stalling.

"I guess I can tell you," the man said, "since you won't be around to tell anyone else. I read an article in the paper about breeders who raise dogs for sale to labs. It said there was good money to be made. The only problem was, I didn't have any start-up cash. There's all that overhead—what it costs to feed and care for the dogs. I figured, hey, steal the dogs, and the overhead will be next to zero." He snickered. "I can get two hundred for a healthy dog. I've got almost five thousand dollars' worth of animals in this first load." He chuckled maniacally at his own brilliance. "It'll make me rich. And even if it doesn't, it sure is better than hosing out dog runs."

Hosing out dog runs. That was it! The dognapper had just told Joe who he was.

"Trent," Joe said, "if you sell those dogs to a lab, Frank and I will be after you until we catch you."

There was silence. Although Joe was in no position to celebrate, he smiled in spite of himself. He had to be right!

127

"What's the matter, Mike," Joe asked, "dog got your tongue?"

"Thanks," Trent said finally. He pulled off the rubber mask. "This stupid mask is too hot anyway. And as soon as I make a phone call, I'll be back to deal with you and the girl. I'm sorry, but you don't leave me any choice."

"Right," Joe said, sarcasm in his tone, "this whole thing is our fault. You really ought to be ashamed of yourself. What kind of lowlife steals people's pets?"

"Rant all you want. It's going to be your last chance," Trent said as he opened the door to the garage.

Even as Trent locked the door behind him, Joe was working his chafed hands free from the tape.

The sun was just rising as Frank pulled up under the portico of the Doghouse Pet Motel. The office door opened with a bang. Dana Bailey rushed out, talking as she ran. Frank lowered the windows so he could hear what she was saying. Dana was apologizing to someone inside, saying it was an emergency, that she had to go home to check on something important.

Frank slid down out of sight. When he peered over the dashboard, he realized he needn't have worried. Dana was in such a hurry that she never even looked his way.

Frank waited until Dana had jumped into the

Doghouse van. Once she was out of the drive and into traffic, Frank pulled out after her. He figured she wouldn't recognize his dad's car. Besides, he had to get to Iola and Joe before it was too late. He knew Dana would lead him right to them.

"Back so soon?" Joe asked when Mike Trent returned to the garage. Trent brought a kerosene lamp with him.

"What's the matter," Joe said, "you break your only flashlight?" Joe twisted the strong tape that bound his wrists. He felt it begin to stretch and weaken. He knew it would come loose eventually, but he wasn't sure there was much time left. "Let me out of here, and I'll get the flashlight in my van."

"Enough chitchat," Trent said. "It's time for me to dispose of you two once and for all. I really don't see any other solution." Trent put the lamp down next to a pile of newspapers.

"You could turn yourself in," Joe suggested.

Trent snorted. "Yeah, right."

Joe watched as the former kennel man removed a small leather kit from his hip pocket. He held it up for Joe to see.

"Curious?" Trent asked.

"I can hardly wait," Joe said.

Trent unzipped the pouch. Joe watched with growing fear when Trent removed a hypodermic needle and a small bottle of clear liquid.

"Sodium pentobarbital," Trent said. "I got this

from the pharmacy at Bayport Community College when I was studying to be an animal technician. Six cc's of this in a sick, aging dog," Trent said smoothly, "and he closes his eyes and never wakes up again. For you, I'll triple the dose, just to be sure."

"Don't you think you're in deep enough as it is?" Joe asked. "You use that drug, you're facing a murder rap."

"Don't be a fool," Trent said. "I'll be long gone. Once I dispose of you two and take the dogs to New York, I'm history, vanished."

"What are you going to do?" Joe asked Trent. "Hide behind rubber masks the rest of your life?"

"I don't have to listen to you," Trent said, "and in a few minutes, you'll have nothing to say."

Joe looked on in horror as the dognapper inserted the needle into the rubber seal in the top of the bottle, then turned the two upside down. He drew half the bottle's contents into the syringe.

"Now," Trent said, "just because I'm a thief doesn't mean I'm not a gentleman." He turned toward the back of the garage, where Iola lay bound and gagged on the old cushions. "Ladies first," he said.

Joe strained against the electrical tape. He watched as Iola tried to push herself away from Mike Trent. Trent bent over her and took the cloth out of her mouth.

"Any last words?" he asked.

Joe saw Iola glare at the dognapper. "Oh, not

talking to me?" Trent said. "You're breaking my heart."

Joe watched helplessly as Trent took her roughly by the arm. He was holding the syringe upright in his other hand.

"There's no point in fighting it," Trent told Iola in a pleasant tone. "As I told your friend, the chemical works very quickly."

Iola looked up at him. Even in the flickering light of the kerosene lamp, Joe could see terror and fury in her eyes.

"It won't hurt a bit," Trent said.

"I've never liked shots," Iola told Trent as he came closer. Spike growled. The dog had been lying quietly at Iola's side.

"Good boy," Trent said to the dog in a soothing voice.

Joe saw Trent lean down again, the syringe poised right above Iola's arm.

Iola has been awfully quiet for the past few minutes, Joe thought. It was much more like her to argue and struggle. He had a feeling she was up to something. He was right.

Suddenly Iola rolled to one side. Joe saw her turn to Spike and yell.

"Spike!" Iola commanded. "Snack!"

Instantly Spike leapt at Trent's upraised arm. The dog's jaws clamped down on the deadly hypodermic, tearing it from Trent's hand.

Startled, Trent let out a shout and recoiled in

fright. At that moment, Joe gave a powerful yank at his wrists, finally breaking the tape. He raced across the room. Grabbing Trent's arm, Joe wrenched it behind the thief's back. This made Trent yell even louder.

When Iola got to her feet, she faced Trent and slapped him hard across the face. Enraged, the dognapper kicked out viciously. His shoe caught Iola in the stomach, knocking her backward. Joe tightened his grip.

Out of the corner of his eye, Joe saw Spike drop the needle. The dog ran barking back into the fight and did his part by biting Trent's ankle. The dognapper howled. But then Spike got between Joe's feet, and Joe went tumbling to the floor.

Trent saw his chance and rushed for the door. In his hurry, he tripped on a garden hose and went sprawling. Joe seized the opportunity to scramble to his feet and lunge for Trent. "Iola," he cried, "let's get him!"

Not many streets away, Frank roared through an intersection. Horns honked and at least one comment on his driving was loud enough that it carried above the screeching of brakes. Frank couldn't help it. Dana Bailey was driving like a maniac. She'd already run two yellow lights and ignored several stop signs. Frank knew if he lost her, Iola and Joe were doomed.

If Dana lied about where she lived, she must have

told other lies, Frank thought as he drove. "Of course!" he said. Frank picked up the cellular phone and dialed the Doghouse. He had to talk to Nora Price. He assumed that was who Dana was shouting to when he saw her racing out of the pet motel. It was too early in the morning for it to be anyone else. Nora answered on the second ring.

While Frank asked Nora Price about Dana's paperwork on the dogs in the kennel, Dana sped through the waterfront district. Frank stayed right with her. Dana didn't slow down until she reached a tree-lined block of old houses. Frank thanked Nora Price for her information, and he hung up.

Dana turned into one of the driveways and parked behind a familiar red pickup. Frank pulled up to the curb. He didn't care if Dana saw him now. He watched her struggle with a large book bag as she got out of the van.

Dana headed behind the house to the garage. She never bothered to look around. Whatever was in the bag she had over her shoulder, it was throwing her off balance. She didn't knock but kicked the door a few times.

"It's me!" Frank heard her yell. "I'm coming in!" Then he saw her reach into the bag and pull something out. Something large. Frank gasped when he realized what it was.

"I've got to stop her," Frank said. "She's got a gun!"

16 Here a Dog, There a Dog

Frank slammed the car door and rushed toward Dana. When he reached the corner of the house, Dana jerked open the door to the garage and disappeared inside.

Frank heard shouts from inside the garage. He sprinted forward, yanked the door open, and stormed inside. His eyes took a moment to adjust to the darkness. What he saw was Iola and Joe standing over Mike Trent, who was pinned to the ground. Spike was chomping on the cuff of Trent's jeans. Trent was kicking frantically, trying to shake the dog loose.

"Get away from him, or I'll shoot!" Frank heard Dana yell. She was aiming straight at Joe's back. As

Frank made a flying leap for the gun, Dana pulled the trigger.

"No!" Iola screamed.

Horrified, Frank saw red splotches burst all over Joe's T-shirt. Covered in crimson, the younger Hardy fought on. Quickly, Frank realized that the gun Dana had fired was a paint gun. It was probably the same gun used against the van right after they had left Excelsior Labs.

"I'm going for the dogs!" Iola shouted. Frank heard her clattering through the garage as he turned his attention to Dana.

When Frank knocked the paint gun out of the Dana's grasp, she hit him with her right fist. She's a lot stronger than she looks, Frank thought, his head reeling back. He tried to grip both her hands, but when she bent down and bit him, Frank immediately let go. Before Frank could stop her, she had swept the gun back up and fired point-blank. Frank shut his eyes. The paint glob hit him squarely in the face. He felt the wetness spread and run down his chin.

Meanwhile, Trent was giving Joe a thorough workout. The younger Hardy was tiring, but he was determined to pay back this creep for all the trouble he'd caused. Locking us in a pet carrier! Joe thought indignantly as he slammed a left to Trent's midsection. Stealing kids' pets! A right to Trent's jaw sent the thief tumbling backward into a pile of

135

shovels and hoes. The tools clattered to the floor, smashing into the kerosene lamp and knocking it over. Trent landed in a wheelbarrow.

Joe ran up to Trent. Just as the dognapper was trying to get up out of the wheelbarrow, Joe socked him hard. The dognapper's head whipped backward, and he slumped back down, unconscious. "Finally!" Joe exclaimed.

Joe's moment of triumph vanished when he turned to see how Frank and Iola were doing. To his horror, he saw the flame from the shattered kerosene lamp licking at a pile of newspapers.

"Fire!" he screamed.

Joe grabbed an empty burlap bag. This garage is a total fire hazard, he thought. He had to put out the fire before it got out of control. He beat the flames repeatedly, stomping the area around the newspapers. He knew that if the fire were to spread, the garage would go up like a tinderbox.

Frank had just wiped the paint from his eyes when he saw the flames. He also saw Dana moving toward the door, clearly trying to escape.

When he determined that Joe had the fire under control, Frank went after Dana. She turned and fired the paint at him again. Once more, he was blinded in a sea of red. This is getting ridiculous, he thought.

Glancing around, Joe saw that he'd smothered the fire before it caught anything. Coughing hard, he peered through the haze of smoke. It billowed upward and quickly filled the open area above the rafters. They might not go up in flames, but if they kept breathing in the kerosene-laden smoke, they could suffocate.

"Frank, Joe," Joe heard Iola call from behind the gray sedan. "I'm letting the dogs out, but I can't find the collie."

Looking around, Joe noticed that there were dogs everywhere. "He's got to be here somewhere," he said.

Joe pushed aside another stack of newspapers. "I found him!" Joe exclaimed. He unlatched the dog's cage and it bounded out of its prison.

Although Frank had never seen the collie that was stolen from the Doghouse Pet Motel, he knew the breed when he saw it. He knew that collies were extremely loyal dogs and would do anything to protect their owners or caretakers. So Frank wasn't surprised when he saw the dog leap across the cluttered floor and get into an attack position right in front of the door. It fixed its eyes on Dana and growled menacingly.

"He's going to hurt me!" Dana cried. She took a step back. The dog growled again and barked, displaying its teeth.

"Mike!" she screamed. Dana was panicking now. "Where are you?"

Frank grabbed the paint gun from her and tossed it across the room.

"Get this dog away from me," she shrieked. She didn't even fight Frank when he grabbed her arms.

"He doesn't seem to like you much," Frank said. He thought the dog had good taste in people. "Don't worry, as long as you don't do anything foolish, the dog won't harm you too much."

"Where's Mike?" Dana wanted to know.

"We'll find Mike just as soon as I call the police," Frank told her. Frank looked at the large garage doors. They were locked shut with brass padlocks. "These fumes can't be doing us or the dogs any good. We've got to air this place out. Do you have the keys to those locks?" he asked Dana.

"Mike's got them," she said.

"Joe!" Frank called to his brother. "Trent has the keys to the garage doors."

"I'll get them," Joe replied.

When Joe returned to the spot where Trent had fallen during the scuffle, the dognapper was just coming to. Joe searched his pockets. The keys to the padlocks were on a ring with Trent's car and truck keys.

Joe and Iola unlocked and opened the large doors while Frank kept hold of Dana.

As soon as the doors were opened the dogs rushed outside, barking and yelping. Iola followed, Spike at her heels. The collie gave Dana a last growl and then bounded outside.

"You can let go of me," Dana said. "To tell you the truth, I'm glad it's finally over."

Frank loosened his grip on the dejected woman. He didn't think she was going to try anything more. "I'm going to call Con Riley from Dad's car," Frank told Joe. Together they walked out of the garage and Frank led her to the car.

Iola joined Joe. "Ahh," she said, "fresh air."

"Did we let all of the dogs out of their cages?" Joe asked.

"Twenty of them in all," she said. Joe saw that the collie was already rounding up the stolen dogs. The collie circled them, then barked out what must have been some kind of order, because Joe noticed that all the dogs stayed in a group.

"Where's Trent?" Frank asked Joe when he came back from calling the police.

"He's still in the garage," Joe said.

Suddenly Joe saw the collie freeze and let out a series of barks. He turned to see Trent appearing out of the shadowy garage interior. Trent was wielding a garden rake.

"You thought you had me!" Trent snarled. He stepped forward and took a swipe at Joe.

Joe neatly sidestepped the blow, and Trent missed by a mile. Spike bounded up to Trent, ears laid back and teeth bared.

The collie barked several times. Joe decided it must be a special dog call, because the other dogs made their way over to Spike and the collie. They surrounded Trent, and Joe could see that not a tail was wagging.

"Call off these dogs," Trent said.

"It's over!" Frank told Trent.

"He's right," Dana said as she walked back from the Hardys' car with Frank.

Trent sagged like a balloon losing its air.

"Sit, Spike!" Frank called. The dog looked up at Frank and cocked its head.

Meekly Trent let the Hardys lead him onto the grass. The collie let out another series of yelps, and Frank thought the dogs all seemed to relax.

"You fool!" Trent yelled at Dana when he saw her. "You led Frank Hardy right to me. Another ten minutes and I'd have taken care of these meddlers. Then I'd have been on my way to the lab in New York."

"Leaving me here, I suppose," Dana said.

"Hey, this was all your idea," Trent said.

"You liar!" Dana bellowed. "None of this was my idea. This was your stupid scheme. And when you stole the collie and the Hardys got in on it, all I did was try to help. But you wouldn't listen. After Price fired you, Mike, didn't I tell you I would stick by you? That job with Maude Macklin was great. But you weren't content with that. No, you were after some kind of get-rich-quick scheme. What was I supposed to do? I didn't want to be a criminal, but I didn't want to lose you either. So I went along."

"Shut up!" Trent snapped.

"You want me to stand by quietly while you pin it all on me?" Dana asked. "Forget it, Mike."

140

"Who suggested we should take Iola's dog?" he asked Dana. "Who said that was the one sure way to get the Hardys off the case?"

"Dana wanted to use Spike as a hostage?" asked Frank.

Trent nodded. "She figured you'd back off."

"That was your big mistake," Joe said. "It just made us work harder to crack the case."

"Well, I sure never told you to demand a ransom," Dana said, "and I sure never told you to kidnap two people."

"I thought Iola could identify me," Trent said. "She tried to rip off my mask last night. What else could I do? And I wanted that ransom money to make sure I got something out of this deal. I thought I'd be able to sell the dogs in a snap, but I was having trouble getting rid of them. I couldn't believe Dr. Skinner turned me down."

"Why didn't you just return Spike and the collie?" asked Joe.

"Collies are smart dogs," Trent replied. "A lab in New York told me they'd pay me a thousand dollars for that dog."

"I warned you not to steal from the Doghouse," said Dana. "Big man, said he could make it look like it wasn't an inside job. Yeah, right."

"You jimmied the lock *after* you came in," Frank concluded.

Trent nodded. "But the cops didn't think of

141

that," he said smugly. "Dana told me everything they said."

"Was your car really in the shop when you came to meet me and Joe in town? And what about those so-called mysterious phone calls to the Doghouse?" Frank asked Dana.

"I made all that up," Dana admitted. "But Shawn Cabot really did ask me out, and he really did talk about closing down the kennel."

"Were you the one searching our van?" Joe asked Trent.

"Yeah," he admitted. "I wanted to see if you'd found any clues. I was pretty sure that card from Excelsior Labs fell out of my shirt pocket when I was struggling with that pit bull at the warehouse. I didn't realize the dog tag hook had dropped out, too."

"You really haven't got any hard evidence against us," Dana told the Hardys. "It's just your word against ours."

Frank was amazed. "Joe and Iola are victims of a kidnapping," he said, exasperated. "Eyewitness testimony is pretty good evidence, I'd say." He guided Trent over to the red pickup truck and searched it. In moments Frank held up the five-hundred-dollar ransom they had paid for Spike. Under the front floor mat, Frank discovered a small vial of liquid. Frank unscrewed the tiny cap and sniffed it. Instantly, he thrust it away. He waved it near Joe.

"Chloroform," Joe said. "That's what he used on me last night at the park."

"That's why I had such a headache when I woke up," Iola said.

"Where'd you get this?" Frank demanded.

"I'm an animal technician, remember?" Trent sneered. "I stole drugs from the school pharmacy when I was in training."

"You hid my brother and Iola in a cave right below the observation deck," Frank said. "And when I went back down the stairs after my flashlight, you dragged them to your truck, which must have been parked somewhere in the trees. If I hadn't been so stupid, I would've caught you then. But you had enough time because I kept going up and down those stairs."

"And the truth is, you didn't have Spike with you last night," Joe added. "You were just going to take the money and run."

Trent nodded.

"Then you brought Joe and Iola here," Frank said. "In all the excitement, did you by any chance listen to the messages on your answering machine?"

"I told you I didn't want that extra phone line in my apartment," Dana told Trent.

"There's a message on your tape from CAT, a fictitious new laboratory that wants to buy dogs from you," Frank explained. "We were already on to you. And if that's not enough evidence for you, I have a drawing in my notebook of the tire tracks left in the warehouse. I'll just bet they match the tires on that gray car."

Trent hung his head. Joe guessed the guy never figured they'd be so thorough or nail him so completely.

"There's still more," Frank continued. "I phoned Nora Price on the way over here. I asked her if Dana had completed the paperwork on all those dogs in the kennel. You know what she said? She asked me, 'All of what dogs?'"

"Since when is it a crime to put off paperwork?" asked Dana.

"When stolen dogs are being hidden at the kennel without the kennel owner's knowledge," Frank said, "believe me, that's a crime."

"Hey, we had to keep them somewhere," Dana complained. "The barking was bound to arouse suspicion. Mike said he had some dog tranquilizers, but he misplaced the bottle."

"I found it, didn't I?" Trent said tersely. "And if I'd had time to drug them all earlier this morning, they wouldn't have been able to help you."

"So Dana was hiding the stolen dogs right under George Price's nose," Frank said.

"Which explains why Dana never put any name tags on their cages," Joe said.

"I couldn't keep the dogs at my apartment," Trent said, "and Dana wouldn't let me leave them here at her apartment until I found the tranquilizers."

"Your apartment was on Water Street?" Frank asked.

"It used to be. I moved to a room in a boarding-house in the same area. Most of my stuff was in storage so that I could take off at a moment's notice. I was following you, and I realized you were going to search my apartment, so I went up the back stairs and waited. When you came in, I gave you the old pepper gas welcome." He snickered.

"What about the pit bull in the warehouse?" Joe asked.

"I stole it out of a yard on the South Side. I had it in a carrier in my car when Dana called me about you two investigating the stolen collie. That pit bull was one dog I never should have stolen," Trent said. "It nearly took my arm off. That's why I left it as a present for you guys."

"Do you know who owns that warehouse?" Joe asked Trent.

"No. I just drove by the place when I lived nearby. The doors were always open. When you were following me after I took your dog, I figured I could lose you if I drove through there. It worked, too."

"And it was you who pushed the dog food over on us at Pet Provisions?" asked Frank.

"Dana called me in the company van and said you were on your way. I came back early from my delivery. When you started through the storage area, I really let you have it." Trent smiled at the

145

memory. "Then I pretended to be arriving when you left the store. I took the rest of the day off so I could stay on your tail."

"So you followed us back to Pet Provisions that night," Frank said, "caught us from behind—"

"And locked you in pet carriers." Trent smiled. "I liked doing that."

Officer Riley pulled up in his cruiser. He parked and hurried up the drive.

"I've got the handcuffs," Riley told Frank and Joe, "if you've got the crooks."

"Right here," Frank said, pointing to Mike Trent and Dana Bailey.

Riley read the two their rights as he put the handcuffs on them.

"Joe and I can return the collie to the Doghouse," said Frank, "but the Humane Society ought to pick up the rest of these dogs. Oh," Frank added, "one of them probably answers to 'Fluffy.'"

"I'll contact the Humane Society," Riley said, "then call the owners when I get back to the precinct house."

Minutes later, Joe drove Fenton Hardy's sedan up the curving drive to the Doghouse. Nora Price got on the phone immediately to the collie's owner.

"George will be so relieved when he gets back from New York," Nora said. "He's made the deal to start our franchising operation. He told me he's even struck a bargain with Alma Morris. We're going to buy her place. And for a very generous price, I might add. George wants to expand the kennel." Then Nora looked at Iola. "We apologize," she said simply. "We'd like you to return to work here."

"Thank you. I'll think about it," Iola said.

Frank, Iola, and Joe continued to discuss the case as they drove to the Hardys' house. "So the fact that Royal Restorations employed Shawn Cabot and owned the warehouse where we ran into that pit bull was just a coincidence," Frank said. "Shawn Cabot had nothing to do with the dognappers."

"That's right, and neither did Alma Morris," Joe said. "I guess she painted her garage windows black to hide the mess—and to keep out snoopers like us," he added with a chuckle.

"One more thing," Frank said as he pulled the car into the Hardys' garage. "We never did find out what Maude Macklin was doing with those used dog carriers in her office."

"Let's ask her," Joe suggested. Once inside the house, he phoned Pet Provisions and asked for Maude. He was put through to the pet supermarket assistant manager.

"They're for our first annual pet show," she told Joe. "And if you've got a pet, you're invited to enter. The prize is a year's supply of kibble."

"I think I've had enough dog food for a lifetime," Joe told her with a chuckle.

The doorbell rang. Frank answered it, wondering what else could possibly happen in one day.

"Oh, I've missed my Spikers so much!" Amy Keith gushed. "Where is he? I want to hug him."

Spike raced from the kitchen, where he'd been eating. He jumped and whimpered and wagged his tail. Amy cooed. "Was he any trouble?" she asked.

"Not a bit," Frank told her. "We hardly knew he was around."

THE HARDY BOYS® SERIES By Franklin W. Dixon

Can superpowers be super-cool?

the secret world of **ALEX MACK**™

Meet Alex Mack. It's her first day of junior high and *everything* goes wrong! Until an accident leaves her with special powers. . .powers that can be hard to control. It's exciting. . .and a little scary!

ALEX, YOU'RE GLOWING!
BET YOU CAN'T!
BAD NEWS BABYSITTING!

by Diana G. Gallagher

A new title every other month!

Based on the hit series from Nickelodeon®

 A MINSTREL BOOK

Published by Pocket Books

1052-04